AS EASY AS A NUCLEAR WAR

SHORT STORIES INSPIRED BY DURAN DURAN SONG TITLES

PAUL CUDDIHY

First published in 2015

Copyright © Paul Cuddihy 2015
Published by Drone Publishing

Cover design: Siobhann Caulfield
Cover photograph: Tony Hamilton
(Special thanks to Joe Hamilton for his enthusiasm
and patience during the photo-shoot for the cover)
Additional artwork: Tam McKinley

ISBN: 1499337507
ISBN-13: 978-1499337501

TO KAREN

You're in my heart, you're in my soul.
You'll be my breath should I grow old.
You are my lover, you're my best friend.
You're in my soul.

TO LOUISE, REBECCA & ANDREW

I wouldn't like to say my music taste is better than yours… but it is.

TO DURAN DURAN

Thank you for the music, the songs I'm singing.
Thanks for all the joy they're bringing.

Track List

1	Rio	1
2	Like An Angel	3
3	Skin Trade	13
4	All You Need Is Now	29
5	Come Undone	35
6	Hold Back The Rain	40
7	Planet Earth	43
8	Of Crime And Passion	66
9	Careless Memories	72
10	Sound Of Thunder	80
11	Girls On Film	89
12	Electric Barbarella	95
13	Save A Prayer	97
14	The Wild Boys	121
15	Someone Else Not Me	132
16	The Chauffeur	139
17	Hungry Like The Wolf	146
18	Last Chance On The Stairway	162
19	Violence of Summer (Love's Taking Over)	164
20	The Reflex	174
21	Ordinary World	184
22	Lonely In Your Nightmare	192
23	A View To A Kill	201
24	Pressure Off	223
25	Is There Something I Should Know	231

PAUL CUDDIHY

The cool thing about reading is that when you read a short story or you read something that takes your mind and expands where your thoughts can go, that's powerful.
TAYLOR SWIFT

I used to take my short stories to girls' homes and read them to them. Can you imagine the reaction reading a short story to a girl instead of pawing her?
RAY BRADBURY

You listen to a piece of music and it will remind you of something – it might make you happy, it might make you sad, but it is very emotive. And I think that Duran Duran have always understood that.
NICK RHODES

PAUL CUDDIHY

Rio

Geeorge W. Bush appeared to me in a dream last night. I was sitting on the front step smoking a cigarette when he drew up in a black limousine and got out. He sat down beside me and pulled at his fingers, snapping them like firecrackers.

"Can I ask you something?" I said.

"Sure, as long as it's not about politics."

"It's not."

"Okay then," he said.

"Michael Moore said you're functionally illiterate. Is that true?"

"No."

"So what are you reading then?"

"Ulysses."

"Is it any good?" I asked.

"It's okay."

George wanted to ask me a question and I thought it only fair to say yes.

"Do you ever wish your life had turned out differently?" he said.

"All the time," I mumbled.

"I always wanted to be the lead singer in Duran Duran," he said with a sigh. "If Simon Le Bon was president, what do you think he'd do?"

"Probably change the national anthem to one of their songs."

"Which one?"

"Rio maybe?"

"Good song," he said and started singing the

chorus, putting his hand on his heart. "That might work." he said and I nodded, even though I wasn't convinced.

He stood up and stretched, then walked back down the path. When he got to the car he turned and shouted.

"Remember, Paul, don't say a prayer for me now, save it 'til the morning after," giving me a salute as he climbed into his car. I didn't even have time to tell him I didn't believe in God.

Like An Angel

Corrina had pink knickers on. I could see them as she crouched down reading a book. They were the colour of bubble-gum. I imagined there was a pattern, perhaps the day of the week embroidered on the front, part of a seven-day set. They would have read 'SATURDAY' unless she didn't bother matching her underwear to the calendar.

"Hi," she said with a smile that made my stomach jump. Embarrassment crept across my face which I tried to conceal behind the stack of books I was carrying. She slowly stood up, holding out a hand.

"I'm Corrina. Nice to meet you."

I made a clumsy attempt to hold out my hand from under the books and our fingertips briefly collided.

"You too," I mumbled.

"Do you not have a name then?"

"What? Sorry. It's Joe."

"Well, hello Joe."

I smiled, sensing that my face was still burning like the fires of hell. She stared at me, cocking her head to one side, her brows occasionally knotting together. Eventually she gave me another smile that I knew I'd never forget.

"I like you, Joe," she said. "You've got kind eyes."

I didn't know what that meant, though I felt them blinking furiously, like they didn't know whether to be flattered or embarrassed.

"Do you work here?" she said.

"Yes."

"Cool."

The books were beginning to weigh heavily in my arms and I slowly placed them on the floor, careful not to let them topple over. I stood up. She was the height of my chin. Her hair was a cocktail of grey and blue, untidily stylish like she'd taken hours of careful preening to ensure it looked as though she'd just woken up.

"I always wanted to work in a book shop," she said, gazing up at me. "Getting to read all these books, any one you want, whenever you want."

"It's not really like that."

"What's your favourite book?"

"My favourite book? God, that's a hard question."

"But if you had to pick just one… a book that I should buy right now. What would it be?"

"I don't know," I said. "What kind of books do you like?"

"I like romances."

"Romances?"

"But not Mills and Boon ones. Proper stories. Like Chocolat. I love that."

"Chocolate?"

"No! Chocolat. The book. I can't remember who wrote it, but it's wonderful."

"I don't know it."

"It's magical and funny and romantic, and it really makes you want to eat chocolate. Lots of it."

She licked her lips like she was mopping up the residue of some chocolate she'd recently eaten, and it made her lips glisten. They curled up into a smile that I couldn't help but replicate.

"I would love a hot chocolate right now," she said.

Before I could reply, I found myself being pulled

along in her undertow towards the café on the second floor. I glanced round. Scott was standing behind the information desk talking to an old woman. I threw him a quick wave which he didn't acknowledge and then disappeared up the stairs. I wasn't due a break for another half-hour and I'd be in trouble if someone spotted me who realised that. It wasn't like I was slipping out the back door for a quick smoke or round to the bookies. I could just say I was taking an early lunch.

I offered to get the drinks but she told me to sit down, dropping her canvas bag on to my lap and making me promise not to answer her phone if it rang. She was halfway towards the counter when she turned back and leant in close to me.

"I know what you were looking at," she whispered with a wink. My face exploded in flames.

Corrina was waiting for me when I came out of the shop at the end of my shift, just like she'd promised. She waved me over to the bench where she sat drinking a bottle of water.

"So how was work, darling?" she said with a laugh.

"I'm glad it's over for another day."

She slipped her arm inside mine and gave it a quick squeeze. I was surprised at the contact, although a ripple of excitement spread out across my body like her touch was a stone which had skimmed the surface of a sleeping loch.

"Have you been sitting here all this time?"

"For a while. I got bored wandering round the shops."

I looked over towards the book shop. It was now

in darkness and the assistant manager was locking the door while a couple of the girls stood waiting for her. One of them was smoking while the other one was texting.

"So what now?" Corrina said.

"I don't know. Are you hungry?"

"I suppose."

"We could get something to eat."

She shrugged and stared away down the street.

"But I'm not too bothered. Maybe we could just have a drink, a coffee even? Or hot chocolate."

"I read a thing about the guy from REM, the singer one," she said. "He just turns up at the airport and looks at the departure board and then decides where to go, right there and then."

"Why?"

"So that he can get peace and quiet to write his lyrics."

"No, why does he decide there and then? Why doesn't he book something up in advance? It's not like he can't afford it."

"Where's your sense of adventure, Joe? Wouldn't it be exciting to just decide on the spur of the moment to go somewhere, anywhere?"

"I suppose so."

"Just like us right now. Why don't we choose to go away somewhere?"

She smiled and I looked at her eyes, blue and full of endless possibilities like a perfect summer's day.

"We could go to New York, London, Paris, Munich."

"Is that not from a song?"

"Caught red-handed," she said with an infectious giggle that sounded like she was being tickled mercilessly. I started laughing too, just as my phone began ringing. Corrina pulled her arm away. I checked the screen before diverting it to voice mail.

"Why didn't you answer it?" she asked.

"I'll get it later."

"You should call her."

"Who?"

"Your girlfriend. Your wife?"

I shrugged.

"What's her name?"

"Eileen. She's my fiancée."

She nodded like she knew all along. I felt awkward, guilty even, like it was something I'd been hiding from her, even though we'd only just met.

The idea of just taking off sounded nice, a crazy sort of nice, but it was easy for a pop star. He was rich, and he wasn't getting married in six weeks' time.

Corrina shivered. "Let's go somewhere warmer."

"What about in there?" I said, pointing to the pub at the corner of the street.

She shook her head. "I want it to be just me and you, but we can't go back to mine, though."

"Why not?"

"We just can't."

"Is it a mess? I don't mind."

"No, it's not that. It's John."

"John? Who's John?"

"My husband."

"You're married?"

She nodded.

"I didn't know you were married."

"Well, you're engaged."

"But your hand. There's no ring."

She laughed.

"How long have you been married?"

"Two years, four months, eighteen days and ..." she glanced at her watch, "... six hours."

We sat on the bed facing each other. I wasn't sure what was supposed to happen next, whether I was meant to lean over and meet her halfway, our lips locking together for our first kiss or whether, if I tried to do that, I'd break the spell and we'd suddenly realise we were just two strangers in a hotel room.

"Tell me something about you," Corrina said.

"Like what?"

"I don't know. Anything. I don't really know much about you."

"Well, I don't know much about you either."

"So tell me your secrets and I'll tell you mine."

I smiled nervously, trying to think of something that would make me sound interesting or exciting.

"I've got an idea," she said, bouncing up and down on the bed. "Every time I take something off I can ask you a question and you have to answer it, and I'll do the same for you ... and it's got to be the truth."

"Are you serious?"

She began to tug at her boots.

"Here, give me a hand," she said, holding her leg out. I gripped the suede boot and firmly pulled it off.

"Looking at my knickers again?" she asked and I quickly turned away. "It's okay, I don't mind," she laughed.

I helped her with the other boot, throwing them both on to the floor.

"Shoes don't count," she said and I discarded mine.

"Okay, who's first?" she asked, looking at me with expectant eyes. I shrugged and peeled off my jumper, rolling it up and lobbing it on to a chair.

"So what's your question?" she asked.

"Why are you called Corrina?"

"Because my dad was a Dylan fan."

I looked puzzled.

"Dylan … Bob Dylan."

"I know who Dylan is but why Corrina?"

"After the song … Corrina, Corrina…" She started singing but I didn't recognise the tune. "My name's Corrina Corrina Donnelly. So good they named me twice."

She asked me if I was happy as she threw her waistcoat at my face. I shrugged, not really sure what she meant. I was happy, right here, right now, and I told her that.

"But what about in general?" she said. "Your job, your life … Eileen?"

"Well, my job's boring and I'm here with you so I don't know what that says about me and Eileen."

"And your life?"

I sighed. That was a big question. I wasn't expecting anything so difficult.

"I don't know," I mumbled. "Are you happy?"

"No question without taking something off."

I started to unfasten my belt and Corrina's eyes widened. I laughed and unbuttoned my shirt instead. She eyed me up and down with exaggerated appreciation, giving me a wolf whistle, and I grinned as I saw myself in the mirror behind her. I wanted to know why she was here with a man she'd caught looking up her skirt. She laughed.

"Are you not scared?" I asked.

"Your eyes are too kind to be dangerous."

That was the second time she'd mentioned my eyes. I started to ask her what she meant but she stopped me. I'd already used up my question. It was her turn again. She lifted her white T-shirt up. A diamond sparkled in her belly button and a Star of David tattoo nestled on her left hip. I wanted to reach over and touch it. When she dropped the t-shirt on to her lap, she folded her arms across her breasts.

"What happened to your back," I asked, looking at her reflection in the mirror.

"It's not your turn," she snapped, snatching up the T-shirt and starting to pull it back over her head. I leant across and stopped her. I wrapped my arms round her. She tried to pull away but I wouldn't let go and her resistance soon evaporated. My fingertips caressed her back, reading the wounded flesh like it was Braille. It described every punch and kick and blow. I could hear a voice that raged, could see an arm raised, heard the swish of a belt through the air and the snap as it hit its target; I felt the silent blows of the buckle. Her breath rippled across my chest as my lips rested on the top of her head. The drone of a television seeped through the wall from the next room but it was too low to guess the programme.

She eventually broke free of my embrace and crawled across the bed, grabbing her T-shirt and disappearing into the bathroom. I could hear running water as I slipped my shirt back on. Pushing the pillows up against the headboard, I sat back and checked my phone. Three voice messages, all from Eileen, but I didn't want to hear them. I kept glancing towards the bathroom door, wondering whether I should go over, but I didn't know what to say.

After a few minutes the door opened slowly and Corrina appeared, eyes red, lips no longer smiling. She jumped on the bed and snuggled in beside me, resting her head on my chest.

"Can I ask you something?" she said.

"Sure."

"Only because you stole my turn last time."

"Okay," I laughed.

She pushed herself up until we were face-to-face. I tried to hold her gaze but blinked first.

"Will you still love me tomorrow?" she asked.

"What?"

"Will you still love me tomorrow?" This time she sang the words as she leant over and placed her lips gently on mine.

"It's okay," she whispered. "Tonight the light of love is in your eyes."

I could only smile, bemused.

I woke up and stretched my arm across the bed. Corrina was gone. My head slowly sank into the pillow. Everything suddenly seemed so predictable again. I would get up and have a shower, then check out the hotel and head home, making sure I got my story right before Eileen quizzed me. She would scream and shout, or storm out, maybe even throwing her engagement ring at me before leaving, but she would forgive me eventually, at some point in the next six weeks, so long as I stuck to my story – whatever it was – and after a while I'd wonder whether Corrina had really existed or not.

I glanced round to where she'd been, where she'd fallen asleep as I watched. Her pink knickers lay on the pillow. I picked them up and grinned as I examined them back and front, noticing the word 'TUESDAY' printed in flowery lettering. Maybe I wouldn't go home after all, I thought, wondering what colour Saturday really was.

Skin Trade

The buzzer above the door announces his entrance. He looks lost, like a child separated from his mother in a busy shopping-centre and standing perfectly still in the hope that he'll be rescued. The look of bewilderment and growing panic is slowly replaced by wonder. He gazes round the shop, at the walls, the ceiling, the floor and then the walls again. His sense of wonder is child-like too, a boy in a toy shop, or Charlie Bucket in Willy Wonka's Chocolate Factory.

On busy days his presence would have gone unnoticed. He might just have been coming in to collect a child – a grandchild more likely, from the look of him – but it is Tuesday morning at half past ten. Valerie knows the time because she keeps checking the Elvis clock on the wall behind her; his arms move to signify the time. At ten to three, for example, he looks like he's singing and striking a classic pose, maybe *Blue Suede Shoes* or *Heartbreak Hotel*? Twenty past three, it's as if he's been punched in the gut and is in the midst of a spasm which has left his lithe body contorted with pain. Half past ten doesn't look too awkward, more like Elvis is in the middle of an exercise regime, one hand reaching up while the other touches his toes.

Valerie flicks through the appointments book. There's one at half past twelve, just a bit of touching up on previous work, while someone is coming in at one o'clock for a consultation, a lunchtime appointment squeezed into a busy working day. Then nothing until half past three. The man slowly approaches the counter, his feet barely leaving the floor.

"Hi," she says.

"I'm Harry O'Connell."

Valerie isn't sure if it is a statement or a question, the inflection in his voice almost searching for affirmation. She holds out her hand.

"Nice to meet you, Harry O'Connell. I'm Valerie Watson."

His smile is as weak as his handshake. It's like he's resting his hand in Valerie's palm. He doesn't immediately let go.

"You have soft fingers," he says.

"Well, I need to look after them, Harry. They're my livelihood."

"They're smooth."

"Thank you."

"Like the skin of an apple."

She gently withdraws her hand.

"How can I help you today, Harry?"

"It's my wife," he says.

"Your wife?"

"I don't want to forget her."

"Why would you forget her, Harry?"

"Rose."

"Her name's Rose? That's a nice name."

"No, that's her favourite flower."

He begins rolling up his jacket sleeve under which is a plain blue shirt that is buttoned. He keeps trying to push the shirt up as well but without any success.

"Here, let me help you," Valerie says, placing one hand on his arm to soothe his mounting frustration while, with her other hand, she unbuttons the shirt and pushes it up, exposing pasty-coloured flesh covered with grey hairs.

"Can you put my wife here?" he says, patting his arm.

"What do you mean?"

"Her name. Angela."

"That's a nice name."

"Can you put it on my arm?"

"You want a tattoo?"

Harry nods.

"Are you sure?"

"I don't want to forget her."

"Why would you forget her, Harry?"

He leans on the desk, letting it take his weight.

"Are you okay," she asks, touching his arm again.

"I don't know."

"I'll get you a seat." She quickly grabs the one from behind the counter and shuffles round 'til she's beside Harry. "Here you go."

He doesn't resist when she nudges him gently towards it and he drops down gratefully.

"Do you want a glass of water?"

Harry nods.

When she gives him the glass, he clutches it with both hands and raises it slowly to his lips like a priest sipping wine from a chalice. As he gulps the cold liquid, some of it dribbles down his chin and on to his shirt. He doesn't seem to notice.

"Do you want more?"

"No thanks," he says, handing the glass back to Valerie. He stares beyond her, above her, behind her. He frowns or smiles, sometimes nods or even raises an eyebrow, and Valerie tries to guess which image has provoked which expression.

"Do you see any that you like?"

"I don't know," he says. "There are so many to choose from."

"Thousands."

"Can you draw them all?"

"Yes."

He whistles slightly as his gaze turns on her. His eyes run up and down the length of her. She doesn't feel awkward or embarrassed. She is used to the attention. It doesn't mean she is beautiful, or that she thinks she is. 'Eye-catching' is how she describes herself. Eyes always follow her, inspect her, undress her, admire her, judge her. She ignores them all. Harry's pupils stop darting and focus in on something. She glances down at herself and then at Harry again. If he was younger, she might have suspected he was just staring at her breasts.

"What's that?" he says, pointing.

She pulls down her dress slightly until the curve of her breast is visible.

"This one?"

Her fingertip grazes the tattoo, a black sledge-hammer shattering a red heart into tiny pieces which are scattered over her flesh.

"What does that one mean?"

"It just reminds me of someone I used to know."

"Is it an old tattoo?"

"A couple of years."

He nods like he knows the story already and she stares at him more closely, frowning slightly. She lets go of her dress and it slips back into place, though part of the sledge-hammer and a few fragments of her heart remain visible.

"Do you already have any tattoos, Harry?"

"No."

"So why start now?"

"I don't want to forget my wife."

"Why would you forget her?"

"Because I forget things nowadays. People's names, their birthdays, where I left my slippers. My pin number."

"I keep doing that too."

"It's not forgetfulness. It's... Well, you're still young. I'm old."

"You're not that old."

"Sixty-three."

"That's not old."

"It's old enough. What age are you?"

"I'm thirty-seven."

"That's young."

"But I'm not getting any younger."

Valerie doesn't feel young though she knows, despite what she sometimes says, that she isn't old. Not yet, but she can feel it creeping up on her, the aches and pains and coughs and colds offering gentle portents, while her empty flat says more in silence than any words could articulate. She might fill the vacuum with voices from the radio, the splash of running water filling a bath, a tuneless reverie as she clumsily sings along to songs she vaguely knows or remembers. She can shout at the top of her voice, have conversations with her reflection about Iraq or the economy, or the wisdom of continuing to dye her hair black when grey hairs lurk under the surface of her skull, but nothing can hide the inescapable fact that she is thirty-seven and on her own.

"So can I get a tattoo?"

"You really want one?"

"Yes."

"And what does your wife think about it?"

"... She thinks it's a good idea."

His hesitation tells her what she needs to know. She straightens up and Harry watches her as she stands at her full height. Five foot ten in flat shoes. She is wearing a pair of emerald green baseball boots. He looks down at them, though it is her legs he is more interested in, the tattoos he can see and the ones which disappear under the hem of her skirt.

"Are you ... Do you ... Tattoos. Are they all over your body?"

"I'm afraid so," she says, stretching her arms out wide and then spinning round, the motion puffing out her dress, giving him a glimpse of what is hidden underneath. "Not quite from head to toe, but near enough."

"Why?"

"Why do I have so many tattoos?"

"Yes."

"I don't know really. It's just happened over the years."

"But you're very pretty."

"Oh."

"No, I mean, you are pretty. Your face. But the tattoos."

"You think they're ugly?"

"No. They're just ..."

"Not pretty?"

"... Different. That's what they are."

"You haven't met many tattooed women, have you, Harry?"

"I've not met any," he laughs. "You're my first one."

"Well, I hope you're not disappointed."

He smiles as he looks her up and down before shaking his head. "No," he mutters.

She moves round to the other side of the counter, hoping he doesn't notice the hint of crimson on her cheeks. She brings out a drawing pad, opening it at a blank page, and lays it on the counter. Then she gets a box of pencils.

"So, first things first, Harry. We need to get a design for you."

"I told you, I just want her name. Angela."

"I know, but you still want it to look nice, don't you?"

"Yes."

"Right, so what I'll do is draw something and you can take it away and show your wife and if you both like it, you can come back in a couple of weeks and I'll do it for you."

"But I want it to be a surprise for her."

"I thought you said your wife thought it was a good idea?"

"She did, but –"

"Well, even if it is to be a surprise, you still need to go away and have a think about it."

"You can't do it right now?"

"Not when it's your first tattoo, Harry. It's a big step, so you need to have a good think about it."

"I have."

"Because once it's done it can't be undone."

"I know. That's why I want it."

As she speaks, Valerie lets the pencil caress the white paper. Black lines soon begin to fill up the page, apparently disparate strokes which are actually interconnected like a complicated system of veins and arteries. After she finishes the outline, she uses different coloured pencils to add substance to the sketch. When she is finished she holds it up for Harry to see.

"What do you think?"

"Roses."

"I thought, since they're your wife's favourite flower, that it would be nice to have them growing within the letters of her name. Do you like it?"

Harry is holding the paper now, staring at it.

"It's beautiful," he whispers, and a tear drops on to the paper. "Oh, sorry. That'll smudge the drawing."

"It'll be fine. You keep that for now. And make sure you show your wife."

Harry doesn't turn up for his next appointment. Valerie isn't surprised, though she's more disappointed than she thought she would be. Either he's forgotten, or more likely he told his wife of his plan and she said no. The appointment was for eleven o'clock, and by half past she's put a line through his name in the appointments book. Just as she does so, the door buzzer sounds and she looks up quickly. A couple of boys in their late teens. They start studying the designs on the walls, pointing and whispering conspiratorially every few minutes. She'll have to ask for proof they're over eighteen when they eventually pluck up the courage to approach the counter. She can vaguely remember being just as nervous when she got her first tattoo. That was many years, and many tattoos ago.

It was a Cupid's Arrow on her hip. She figured at

the time – she was only sixteen – that it was the most discreet spot, where she could look at it whenever she wanted but no-one else would see it unless she revealed it to them. It was a bow with an arrow attached, its tip hidden within a red heart. It was her first heart, but it wouldn't be her last, and at least this one wasn't broken. There had been a boy – wasn't there always? His name was Stuart and he was twenty-one. It was his idea to get the tattoo. She hadn't needed much persuading, excited by the thrill of doing something her parents would disapprove of, and desperate to please her boyfriend because he was five years older and he had a car and all her friends were envious of her. She'd already had sex with him, so what was a tattoo in comparison? She couldn't have articulated it at the time, but even as the needle began carving into her skin, she knew it would last longer in her life than Stuart. Much longer. The shattered heart was someone else's fault, and it was less painful to think of her teenage self than to remember anything more recent.

Her fingers automatically touch her hip, though she's not sure she'd still be able to find Cupid. For one thing it will have faded, and it has been crowded out by other images of varying shapes, sizes, colour and quality, each one with its own individual story, only some of which she remembers. The ones that matter, she does, but that's not always a good thing.

She doesn't hide the tattoos. What's the point of having them if no-one else gets to see them? She wears sleeveless dresses or, when it's very hot or she feels bloody-minded, denim shorts and a vest top, much to her mum's disapproval. Her flesh is covered with random patterns and intricate designs; the crucified Christ, a devil fornicating with an angel, the solar system, a soaring eagle and a venomous snake, a flaming guitar and Jessica Rabbit. A shattered heart.

She calls him sledge-hammer man, if she calls him anything at all. It's a good name for him. Well, a polite one at least. She doesn't want to say his name, or even think it. The sound of it still hurts like a cigarette burn. She was old enough to have known better. At least the tattoo will remind her next time, though she has no intention of there being a next time.

She's working on a tattoo when someone comes into the shop. It's a Latin inscription – Habeo Deum Iudicem. 'God is my judge.'

"I checked it on Google," the girl tells her and Valerie isn't going to argue, or even check for herself. She doesn't care. It's not her tattoo. The girl is lying on her back as Valerie works on the intricate lettering. She wants it on her heart, though she winces a few times as the lettering is etched into her skin. Her eyes are closed which Valerie prefers so that she can concentrate on her work.

"Val, there's someone here to see you." Ryan's head appears round the door and the girl's eyes open to see who has spoken.

"Who is it?"

"Don't know. She wouldn't say."

"Tell her I'll be about half an hour if she wants to come back."

She starts working on the tattoo again, tracing over the 'cem' of the last word. The lettering looks good, she thinks, though without any sense of vanity. She knows that no matter what she is asked to do, the end product will be of the highest quality. That can't disguise the fact that some choices are just awful. She hates doing people's names. Boyfriends or girlfriends. Husbands or wives. True love etched into flesh for all eternity. Don't do it, she wants to scream. It will never last, and even if it does, you'll still look in the mirror one day and wonder who the stupid person with the tattoo is who stares back at you. She says nothing, of course. She just takes the money.

The tattoo is finished. The girl sits up and studies it, a smile breaking out across her face like sun from behind the clouds.

"It looks magic," she says.

Valerie wraps a layer of cling film over it and hands her a jar of Bepanthen.

"Do you know what to do?"

"I think so. It's been a while since my last one."

"Keep the cling film on for an hour. Then take it off and wash the tattoo with soapy water, but when you're drying it, make sure you don't rub it.

"Will it come off?"

"No," Valerie laughs, "but it might smudge a bit."

"Okay."

"Then use the cream, just a little bit. And then wrap it in cling film again tonight and do the same thing again tomorrow. Put cream on it every day until the tattoo's healed. Just follow all the instructions in the leaflet and you'll be fine."

Valerie follows the girl back out to the front of the shop and leaves her to pay Ryan, who stands leaning on the counter beside the cash till. He glances up and nods towards a woman who is sitting in the waiting area. When the woman sees Valerie, she stands up.

"Hi, can I help you?"

"I'm Mrs O'Connell."

"Sorry, do I know you?"

"I'm Harry's wife," she says.

"Harry?... You mean, Harry that wanted the tattoo?"

"Yes."

"You're Angela?"

"Yes."

"Nice to meet you. I'm Valerie."

She holds out her hand and Angela takes it in hers. They both smile politely. Angela's younger than Harry, much younger. She is small and pretty, with bright red lips and eyes dark as a forest. She brushes her shoulder-length hair away from her face and smiles again. Valerie keeps looking away, though her eyes are drawn back to Angela's face.

"I'm from the Philippines," she says.

"I'm sorry. I didn't mean to..."

"It's okay. I get it all the time. I'm used to it now."

"I'm sorry," Valerie says again.

Angela's gaze soaks in every detail of Valerie's body. She waits until Angela's eyes have exhausted themselves and return to looking at her face.

Sorry," she mutters.

"It's okay. I get it all the time too. I'm used to it now," Valerie says with a smile. "So how can I help you? Has Harry told you about his tattoo plan?"

Angela opens her handbag and brings out a sheet of paper, crumpled and creased like a shirt stuffed at the bottom of a wardrobe. Valerie can make out the design she sketched for Harry.

"He wanted that tattoo so he wouldn't forget you."

"I know."

"But he didn't turn up for his appointment. I thought that maybe he told you and you wouldn't let him."

"He's dead."

"What?"

"Harry. He's gone."

Angela starts crying and instinctively holds up the sheet of paper to her face like it is a handkerchief, though as soon as its rough surface touches her skin she moves it away.

"I'm sorry," Valerie says. "Do you want to sit down?"

"I don't know."

"Come on through to the back of the shop and I'll make us both a cup of tea."

She guides Angela gently through to the office that holds a desk, two chairs and not much else. When she brings the tea into the office, she hands one mug to Angela and puts the other one on top of the desk.

"I'm really sorry," she says.

"Thank you."

"I didn't know he was ill."

"He wasn't. It was just so sudden."

"I only saw him a couple of weeks ago."

"Was that when he came in for his tattoo?"

"I told him to have a think about it, or talk to you, and then come back."

"He had dementia, you know."

"He told me. I didn't realise it was so bad."

"It wasn't."

"So what happened?"

Angela takes a gulp of her tea and then puts the mug down beside Valerie's.

"He stepped out on to the road and a car hit him. It just doesn't seem real, no matter how many times I say it. I keep expecting him to walk in through the front door."

She starts crying again, burying her head in her hands. Valerie doesn't move.

"I'm all alone now," Angela says. "I've got no-one."

"What about your family?"

"They're all back in the Philippines. I don't want to go back there."

"What about Harry? Does he have a family?"

"They hate me."

"Why?"

"Why do you think?"

Valerie shrugs.

"He was sixty-three. I'm thirty-seven. I'm from the Philippines. He's from Scotland."

"Is that why they hate you? Because you're younger?"

"They think I'm after his money."

"Who?"

"His kids. His son and daughters. They think Harry bought me and I'm only here for his money. They call me the catalogue bride, and now that he's dead, they believe I'm just a gold-digger who'll run off with their dad's money. They don't even want me at the funeral."

"That's terrible. You're his wife."

Angela brings the piece of paper out again and spreads it on the desk.

"He wanted to put me on his body because he didn't want to forget me."

"I know. He told me."

"That means he loved me."

"He did. He told me that too."

"And I loved him. They don't believe me but I did. I don't care about the money. I just wish I could have him back."

The door swings over behind them and closes. Valerie automatically turns round when she hears the noise. It feels cold, though she's not sure if it is the temperature or the fact that there's a dead body lying in the middle of the room. Angela strides over to the coffin, leaning in and kissing her husband. Valerie remains by the door.

"I don't know if I can do this," she says.

"But you promised."

"I know, but it's wrong."

"It's fine. He's my husband."

"I know, Angela, but still..."

"Please."

Valerie walks slowly over to the coffin, each step forward weighed down with reluctance. Harry looks as though he is sleeping, though the make-up on his face reminds her that he isn't. Angela is already rolling up his right sleeve.

"We've got half an hour. That's all they've given me to say goodbye to my husband. Will you be able to do it?"

Valerie's bag is open and she perches a bottle of ink on top of Harry's chest.

"I'll do what I can, but I don't know what I'll be able to manage in half-an-hour."

There's no time to go through her usual preparations, much of which are hygiene-based, but

Harry is dead so it doesn't matter. Angela has put the design beside the ink bottle and Valerie glances at it as she begins drawing, though the image is planted firmly in her mind since she spent the past couple of days studying it. The quicker she is able to do it, the better. Much of the intricacies of the original idea have been dispensed with, though Angela has insisted that one red rose remains, entwined in her name.

"For love," she says softly and Valerie nods, thinking of her own shattered heart.

As she carves 'Angela' on to Harry's arm, Valerie can hear tiny sobs beside her above the buzz of the gun, but she ignores them, working quickly but carefully. She wants to make sure it's something that Harry would have been proud of. Maybe he would have forgotten who Angela was one day, but perhaps his heart would have always remembered even if his brain didn't? Now she will be there with him, on him, for all eternity.

You never know when you'll fall in love. It could happen tomorrow, Valerie's mum tells her during strained telephone calls. Valerie doesn't really believe it, but sometimes it is a hopeful, if deluded, thought to console herself with.

All You Need Is Now

What's for you won't go by you," David's
mother always used to say to him. He
believed her, too, and why wouldn't he?
The words seemed to make sense. He'd thought of
those words again when she phoned him.

"Rachel's dead," she said.

He was surprised by the measured tone in her
voice. He would have predicted wailing and barely
coherent words gushing down the line.

"Rachel's dead?" he asked.

He wanted to say the words for himself, trying
them on for size as if somehow, by saying them out
loud, it would help his brain comprehend the news. It
didn't help.

"Are you okay, son?"

"Are you okay?" he asked.

There was silence on the other end of the
telephone for a few moments.

"Rachel's dead," she repeated.

Rachel's dead. It sounded strange in his head,
surreal even, like his mother had told him the River
Clyde was made of chocolate or that dinosaurs were
alive and well and living in the Campsie Hills. She
might as well have told him that his father was still
alive. She didn't. Instead, she said that Rachel was
dead.

"How?"

"It was a car crash."

"A car crash? But Rachel's an excellent driver."

"It wasn't her fault," his mother said. "A lorry ran

29

into the back of her. It was trying to overtake her on the Clydeside Expressway. She didn't have a cha...nce."

Her voice just about managed to get the sentence out before the tears began. He let her sob. It was a strangely comforting sound.

He knew the road. They had driven it a thousand and one times together. Sometimes he drove. Other times Rachel did. She was the better driver, though he was always loathe to admit that to her. It had come easily enough to him now, when he spoke to his mother. He closed his eyes and a solitary tear squeezed out, trickling down his cheek, caressing his skin like the tender touch of a lover. Rachel.

"You should phone her parents." His mother's voice was quivering now.

"Okay, I will."

He didn't know what he would say to them. What could he say when they had just lost their only child, their beautiful daughter? He had spent almost as much time in their house as he had his own.

"You're the son they never had," Rachel would joke.

"Does that not make what we do wrong then?" he'd say, raising his eyebrows. She'd laugh, a joyous, uplifting sound that always made him think of sunny, and not so sunny days on the beach at Ayr, and then gently punch his arm. He'd lean in close and kiss her, their lips lingering together like long-lost soul-mates that never wanted to be separated again. More tears began pouring down his cheeks.

"David, are you okay?" his mother asked.

"I don't know."

"I don't like you being so far away. You should be

here with your family at a time like this, not thousands of miles away on your own."

"I'm not on my own."

"Who are you with?"

"Friends."

"But it's not family."

"I'll be fine. Don't worry about me."

"But I do worry, David. Your fiancée is dead and you should be here, with us. I wish you'd never gone there."

David sighed. He didn't want a repeat of previous conversations, ones that never went anywhere or resolved anything. She hadn't wanted him to go to America, something she never tired of reminding him about.

"But it's only for a year," he'd said. "Less than that. The course lasts from September to June, and I'll have three weeks off in December when I can come home."

His mother had frowned, and not even Rachel's easy touch on her shoulder was able to soothe her.

"It will be fine," Rachel had said. "He'll be back in no time."

Rachel would rather he had stayed. So would he, if truth be told, but it was a one-year placement at the University of Iowa that would help with his degree, and his career, and their future...

"I'll be fine, mum," David said. "I'll call Rachel's parents as soon as you hang up."

"Do you want us to book your flight from here?"

"No, I'll book it."

"Martin said that he'll do it. He'll email you the details ... What's that? Hold on a minute, David."

He heard his brother's voice in the background,

asking questions, giving instructions, probably with his laptop perched on his legs, checking details of flights to Glasgow.

"Is tomorrow okay?" she asked.

"That's fine."

"Okay. Martin will email you once it's all booked. Are you sure you'll be okay, David?"

"Yes!"

"It's just so sad. I can't believe it. Rachel."

David stood at the window and looked out through the tear-stained glass. The sky, grey and sickly, was spewing out relentless sheets of rain that battered the building. It had been like that when he woke up and it looked as if it would remain the same for the rest of the day. It reminded him of home, but that didn't bring any comfort. He shivered. He could feel the cold wind through the thin pane of glass and realised he should have put a t-shirt on before getting up. He pressed his forehead against the glass. It was cool and soothing like the underside of a pillow.

It was half past seven. He had to be at the airport by eleven for his flight to New York and then a long wait for a connecting flight home. It didn't feel like home any more. Already. Not without Rachel there, waiting for him. What was he going home for? To say goodbye to her. To watch as she was lowered into the ground, showers of tears and rain falling on the coffin. Then he'd pick up a handful of dirt and drop it on top of the wooden box. It would be the last thing they'd ever do together. Even the thought of the dirt running through his fingers made him wipe his hands now as if he was cleaning them, erasing all trace of something he knew he'd never be able to forget. He didn't want to go back. He knew he had to, but it felt like he was stepping into his past now. Rachel was gone, and he'd never hear her voice again, or her laugh, which he'd always been able to provoke. He'd soon forget the feel of her lips on his, or her body pressed against him. Would there be a day when he'd wake up and not remember anything?

A car horn sounded and he stared down at the street, which the rain had turned mourning black. A delivery van had been abandoned on one side of the road, its hazard lights flashing to signify it had come to a stop. It didn't appease the traffic behind, and one angry horn was swiftly followed by another and another. None of them made the truck move.

He stood for a few minutes, his head still pressed again the glass, eyes closed, Rachel's laughter hovering in the background; the imprint of their last kiss. He ran his tongue along his lips, trying to remember her taste. He breathed in deeply and he could smell her pressed close to him, whispering 'I love you,' at Glasgow Airport as they waited for his flight.

He opened his eyes and re-focused on the street below. The van still remained in place as the driver shuttled back and forth with crates for one of the shops. David presumed it was for the Italian deli. Cars were warily edging their way round its bulky frame, depending on the oncoming traffic. All the while the rain continued falling.

"Are you coming back to bed? It's freezing?"

David turned round. Amanda stood in the doorway, a cover wrapped round her, but he could see she was shivering too.

"I'll just be a minute."

"Hurry up! I need warmed up," she laughed as she disappeared back into the bedroom. It was a short laugh, almost like a dog barking. He told her she smoked too much but she just barked at that too.

"What's for you won't go by you," his mother always told him. She was right too. He could have been in the car with Rachel and then his mother would have been mourning him too.

He had thought that last night as he kissed Amanda, their tongues colliding as they sought out each other's mouths. He'd thought it as his trembling fingers cupped her breasts and his lips sucked on her hard nipples, and when his tongue had drawn a thin line of saliva from her breasts to the triangle of hair where he disappeared, content to hear her occasional sigh or feel her hand grip his hair.

He thought of that as she disappeared under the cover and took him in her mouth, only stopping when he pulled out, afraid of exploding if she kept for going for any longer. He had thought of it when he did explode inside her, biting his tongue to stop from screaming out 'Rachel' as he made one final thrust, groaning loudly at the same time and pushing until there was nothing left in him.

"Are you crying?" Amanda had asked as she sunk on to the bed, lying flat out on her front.

"Sweating," he said, as another drop fell on her back. He was glad she wasn't able to see his face because, in truth, he couldn't tell whether it was sweat or tears that were falling.

"Just sweating," he whispered, rolling over until he lay beside her, kissing her cheek as he did so.

Come Undone

When he saw the death notice in the paper, John knew he had to go to the funeral. He wouldn't be expected, and definitely not welcome, but he felt it was the right thing to do. For him. He was surprised at his own reaction as he read it. He didn't laugh or allow himself a satisfied smile, even though at one point in the not-too-distant past he would have headed to the pub for a celebratory pint. All he could think about now was Elaine.

He thought of phoning his ex-wife but knew his voice wouldn't be one she wanted to hear. The last time they spoke it had gone badly; screaming he hated her and hoped that she and Allan both die horrible and painful deaths hadn't been the wisest thing to say. That had been a year ago.

He had seen her since then, when he parked outside her office or drove past the house, glimpsing her as he slowed down. He'd phone as well, never saying anything, just satisfied to hear her voice. It always sounded best when she was tired, usually in the middle of the night. Allan would come on the line and shout at him but still he didn't say anything. They got a court order in the end and he decided to leave them alone. He was a coward at heart.

He was only going to pay his respects. That's what he told himself. His mum would probably think he was only there to make sure Allan was dead. Elaine would feel the same. He was part of her past and Allan had been her present and meant to be her future. Now she was on her own. Just like him.

It had happened so suddenly, or so it had seemed. One day they were married, the next she had left him. He'd heard Allan's name mentioned before when Elaine was talking about her work but hadn't thought anything of it.

"We're in love," she whined like an infatuated teenager. He wanted to hit her but that would only lessen any guilt she might have felt. She stood with her coat on and a suitcase at her feet, looking like a movie cliché.

"You're pathetic," he said.

She laughed. "No, it's you that's pathetic, John. Pathetic and boring and fat and repulsive."

She snatched up her case and strode out, slamming the front door behind her. He stood in the living room for a couple of minutes before swinging a foot at their wedding picture on the coffee table, sending it flying across the room, scattering shards of glass on to the carpet.

He parked outside the chapel. It was a cold and bright morning, and the sun bouncing off the snowy ground was dazzling. The car park was full, with a hearse and two black limousines parked nearest the door. Two undertakers leant against a wall having a smoke while a third was wiping the bonnet of the hearse with a cloth. They hadn't noticed him and he checked himself in the rear-view mirror one last time. He smiled. He couldn't help it. And when he smiled that made him laugh.

He sunk down under the dashboard and put on the bright orange wig, adjusting it so that the nylon curls weren't draped down over his face. Taking a deep breath he opened the door. He would have to be quick. There was no time for second thoughts, or any thoughts. The undertakers looked up at the sound of the car door slamming shut. One of them nearly choked on his cigarette as John ran past them. He squeezed his nose as he did so, the horn sound startling them.

He wore a bright red silk suit splattered with a kaleidoscope of colours like a group of nursery school kids had attacked it with paint brushes. He'd thrown on a white t-shirt but no-one would notice because of the giant snot-green bow-tie round his neck. As well as the wig, he'd got his face painted; white with a fake red smile like The Joker in the Batman films, black eyes with a couple of tears dotted on his cheeks. And the nose, like a bright red ping-pong ball.

The woman at the fancy dress shop had painted his face. She felt sorry for him when he told her there was no-one else to do it. He could have worn the massive shoes as well but decided trainers would be better in the snowy circumstances. Gliding past a couple of men wearing white sashes who stood at the back of the chapel, he slid open the door and sprinted up the aisle.

"Here's Johnny!" he shouted, giving his nose another toot. Heads turned and the priest stopped talking. There was complete silence. Even the crying seemed to have evaporated.

Reaching the coffin, he plunged his hand into the jacket pocket and brought out a toy Santa Claus, which he wound up. He set it on top alongside a framed picture of Allan and Elaine. He shrieked as Santa started moving across the glossy wooden surface, the strains of *Jingle Bells* filling the building.

He jumped up on the altar and headed for the priest, who started to back off. John honked his nose again and squeezed the bow tie, firing a spray of water into the priest's terrified face. The old man stumbled as his hands shot up to his face and John could hear gasps from the congregation.

"Always look on the bright side of life!" he sang as he darted across to the altar, snatching up the chalice and taking a drink of the wine, some of the dark liquid dribbling down his chin. He screwed up his face. 'Waiter, this Buckfast is corked!'

Jumping down from the altar, he noticed a couple of men who'd squeezed out from one of the rows heading towards him and he grabbed a bouquet of flowers from a vase at the side of the coffin, throwing them in the air with another shriek. Elaine was sitting, head in hands, her shoulders shaking uncontrollably while a young man John presumed was one of Allan's sons had his arm round her. Santa was still playing *Jingle Bells*.

"Cheer up, it might never happen!" he shouted as he darted towards the side door, bursting out into the cold air and colliding with one of the undertakers. He squirted him with water from the bow-tie and sprinted for his car, jumping on the bonnet of the hearse as he did so, leaving a dent in the shiny black metal. He was glad the church car park had been gritted.

The engine was still running as he dived into his car, ignoring a group of children who'd gathered outside the chapel in the mistaken belief it was a wedding and there would be a scramble after the service.

"Do you juggle, mister?" one boy shouted.

"All the time, son. All the time," John muttered, letting off the handbrake and pressing the accelerator to the floor.

Hold Back The Rain

I saw Andy Taylor walking into my local supermarket the other day. I don't want to tell you which one because I don't like to give the bastards any free publicity, and if I said where it was they'd chase me next time I turned up there with my guitar and started playing outside, because they're bastards.

I was in the middle of a song, *I Will Always Love You* – the Dolly Parton original, obviously, not that woeful Whitney Houston version – when I saw him walking across the car park. For a moment I was almost distracted enough to forget what I was singing, but I managed to keep it together so that no-one noticed. The words kept coming out of my mouth in time to the music, but in my head I kept hearing, 'Fuckin' hell. There's Andy Taylor, the former lead guitarist with 1980s pop band, Duran Duran.' I cut the song short as he reached the front door.

"Andy! Andy!" I shouted but he either didn't hear me or he ignored me as he disappeared inside the shop. I hoped it was the former because I hate it when famous people are like that, acting all big-headed and ignoring you just because they're rich and you're busking out in the cold while a wee drunk woman dances in front of you in time to a different beat.

Carol Vorderman totally blanked me once, even when I told her I preferred her on Countdown to Rachel Riley. That's not true, though Carol wasn't to know that.

I decided to have a rest and wait until Andy came back out of the shop, so I sat down on the speaker and rested the guitar on my lap. I had a Star Bar in my pocket which seemed quite appropriate, and I nibbled it because it would be a while before I ate again.

When I saw Andy I was going to tell him that he was the reason that I started playing guitar. Famous people like it when you pander to their ego. That wasn't true either. It was really Val Doonican.

I saw him on the telly when I was only about six. He was playing the guitar and singing – I don't remember the song – but it sounded amazing and I decided right there and then that that's what I wanted to do. It's unlikely I'll ever see Val around here to tell him, though. I don't even know if he's still alive, but if I did see him, I'd tell him that *Paddy McGinty's Goat* is one of the greatest songs ever written, and I wouldn't be making that up.

After about twenty minutes, Andy Taylor reappeared clutching a carrier bag. I couldn't make out everything that was in it, but a big plastic bottle of Irn Bru was sticking out the top.

"Andy!" I shouted, standing up. "Andy mate. You're a legend."

He was coming towards me but still he didn't smile or nod or even acknowledge me.

I started playing *Hold Back The Rain* and singing. He glanced briefly in my direction but kept walking.

"Andy Taylor?" I said, stepping out in front of him.

"Sorry pal, you must have the wrong guy."

"You're not Andy Taylor?"

"No."

"From Duran Duran?"

"No."

"You're a dead ringer for him."

"Sorry."

He walked round me and headed back towards his car. I followed him and noticed that he got into a black Corsa. It wasn't really a rock star's car, but it might have been his wife's. I could have sworn it was definitely him, though when I thought about it later, I remembered that the band were English and my Andy Taylor definitely had a Glasgow accent.

Planet Earth

W
here are you going?" Mick asked.

Danny glanced at the map he'd been given. "The English Department."

"Boring!"

"Why, where are you going?"

"The Russian Department."

"The Russian Department?" Danny laughed. "What are you going there for?"

"Because they give you free tea."

"Free tea?"

"Iced-tea."

"Iced-tea? You don't even know what it tastes like, and you don't know any Russian."

"It'll just be cold tea with ice in it," said Mick. "That's good enough for me, comrade."

"You don't know if they give you tea."

"They do," said JP. "My cousin told me they got it last year. They all sat pretending they were interested in studying Russian so they could get some tea."

"They'll know you're not interested."

"They don't care," said JP.

"But what's the point?"

"It's free tea," said Mick.

"And you get oranges and lemons in it as well," said JP.

"So you've come here just for some free tea?"

"It's an afternoon off school," said Mick.

"Well, I'm going to the English department."

"What for?"

"Because you get chocolate biscuits if you tell

them you want to do an English degree. Blue Ribands, I think."

"Do you?"

"No, you fuckin' don't." Danny shook his head.

"So why are you going there then?"

"Why do you think?"

Mick shrugged.

"Because I want to study English."

"English is shite," said Mick. "All that reading and Shakespeare stuff. I don't understand any of it."

"Well, that's where I'm going." Danny moved away, glancing at the map again and trying to figure out which way he should be going.

"So are you not coming with us then?" Mick shouted after him. "It's free tea!"

Danny kept walking, letting the words float up into the air and dissolve. He was going to university. There was no discussion in the house that he might do anything else. To be fair to his parents, he wanted to go. Frances was already there. She was studying French and Spanish, and he was expected to follow in her footsteps, though he wouldn't be doing a languages degree. The only issue up for debate was the choice of university. Danny wanted to go to Glasgow. It looked like a real university. It felt like one too, as he crossed the road and headed through the archway and into the quadrant which led towards the English Department.

The place was full of students, some of them moving between classes – lectures – while others stood in small groups, chatting and smoking and laughing and no doubt discussing the political issues of the day, which would conclude with universal agreement that Thatcher was a cow. Danny was conscious of the fact he stood out. He wished that the headmaster hadn't insisted everyone wore their green school blazers.

Signs pointed towards the English Department and there were a few other people who looked similarly uncertain of their surroundings heading in the same direction, so he followed in their wake. Maybe he'd end up sitting in lectures with some of them?

There were three girls, all wearing brown blazers that could only be described as the shade of shite, and he remained a few steps behind them as they followed the signs, pointing each one out gleefully as they spotted it and then moving on excitedly like they were on a treasure hunt.

Danny tried not to smile as he studied them. They were all different heights, and seemed to have positioned themselves as such, from smallest on the left to tallest on the right, with the chubby one in the middle. They all wore the same brown, billowing skirts which matched their blazers, though he did like the fact the smallest of the three girls was wearing a pair of sannies rather than shoes. He hoped she'd be the prettiest of the three. They pushed their way through a set of swing doors and disappeared inside a building. They didn't check to see if anyone was behind them, and Danny stopped as the doors swung back viciously towards him. When they settled down, he pushed through them and stepped into a corridor. The three girls were nowhere to be seen. There were no signs pointing him in the right direction either, and Danny found himself paralysed for a moment, glancing up and down the corridor helplessly.

He began walking up the stairs rather than head

along the ground floor corridor. He reached the first floor landing and then stopped again, looking along an identical corridor to the one below. It was empty too, and there were no signs. He wondered where the three girls had gone. He heard footsteps behind him and glanced round. A girl was walking up the stairs, her head bowed like she was studying her feet to make sure she didn't trip over. She had almost reached the top when she glanced up, and looked startled at Danny standing in front of her. She took a half-step back and Danny was worried that she was going to topple down the stairs. She seemed to steady herself and then held his gaze.

Dyed black hair fell over her eyes and she kept blowing it away out the side of her mouth. Her lips were painted purple, though she didn't have much make-up on the rest of her face. She wore a black t-shirt underneath a black leather biker's jacket. Her denim skirt was shorter than any skirt Danny had seen the girls at Saint Angela's wear while her legs were covered by heavy black tights which disappeared into a pair of Doc Martens. There was a denim bag slung over her shoulder, the material barely visible underneath the felt-tip pen scrawls and badges which seemed to cover just about every inch of the bag. It was the badge on her jacket which impressed Danny the most. Joy Division. She was a student. A real, live, female student. His mouth suddenly felt dry and he swallowed hard a couple of times to try and regain some power of speech.

"Do you want a picture?" she said.

"What?"

"Did you get a good enough look?"

"Sorry, I... eh... English..."

46

"What are you jibbering about? Do – you – not – speak – English?"

"No, it's just…" Danny coughed to clear his throat. "I'm looking for the English Department."

"What part?"

"What part of what?"

"What part of the English department? Are you sure you speak English?"

"What do you mean?"

"Well, is it contemporary European literature? Is it nineteenth century British literature, or the early British novel?"

"I don't know. Just the English department."

"You could get a good heat off that face," the girl said, laughing as she held out her hands towards Danny. He knew he was blushing and he began to move away.

"Wait a minute," the girl said and he stopped. "Do you like Dickens?"

Danny shook his head and started walking again.

"Wait! Have you read any Charles Dickens?"

Danny nodded.

"What have you read?"

"Great Expectations."

"Well –"

"And Oliver Twist." Danny lied, though he had seen the film and he thought he'd be able to bluff it if she quizzed him about it.

"Did you like them?"

"They were okay."

"Okay?"

Danny shrugged.

"The best English novelist of all-time and your assessment is that he's okay."

Danny moved away with a sigh.

"Wait," the girl said, tugging on his sleeve to stop him. "Sorry, I'm only teasing. I'm going to the nineteenth century British literature class if you want to start there." She pointed along the corridor and Danny glanced in that direction.

"Okay."

The girl smiled and started walking. Danny stared straight ahead. He knew his face was still red and he didn't want the girl to catch him looking at her again. He breathed in and managed to steal a glance at her. She smelt of strawberries.

"I'm Caroline," she said. "What's your name?"

"Danny," he mumbled.

"Nice to meet you, Danny Dickens." She laughed as she held out her hand and he shook it weakly. He noticed her nails were painted the same shade as her lips.

Their footsteps echoed up and down the corridor. Well, Danny's did and he wished he'd worn his trainers rather than the shoes his mum had insisted he put on. "You want to make a good impression," she'd said as she polished the shoes. He knew the only impression he was making now was that he was just a stupid schoolboy walking beside a smart student.

"So are you coming here then? Caroline asked.

"I don't know. Hopefully."

"You need to wait on your results?"

Danny nodded.

"It's the best English department," she said. "Much better than Strathclyde."

"So I heard."

They were about halfway along the corridor when the three girls Danny had been following appeared out of one of the rooms. The tallest girl was leading the way, and Danny was slightly dismayed to notice that it was the chubby girl who was the best-looking. He knew it wouldn't put off some of his pals. "Why look at the mantelpiece when you're poking the fire," Mick would say. Danny didn't believe that, though he never said anything. He also didn't believe Mick had poked any fires, attractive or ugly ones.

Caroline knocked on the door and opened it. There was a name plaque stuck on the front of it, with 'Professor James Graham' engraved on it. Underneath was a handwritten piece of paper. 'NINETEENTH CENTURY BRITISH LITERATURE'. Danny followed Caroline, closing the door behind him.

It felt like a small room, though in truth it was hard to tell since it was full of books. Three of the walls had book-cases crammed with books, folders and paper. There were stacks more piled up on the floor, while the large desk which sat underneath the window looking out on to the quadrant Danny had crossed earlier, was also covered with books and papers. A man sat at the desk. He was reading a book, but immediately put it down still open at the page he'd been reading, on what seemed to be the only bit of the wooden desk still visible.

"Sit down, sit down," he muttered, pointing to the couch in front of one of the book-cases. Both Danny and Caroline lowered themselves slowly on to the seat. "I'm Professor Graham," he said.

He took off his glasses, holding them to his mouth and breathing on them before wiping the steamed-up glass with the sleeve of his cardigan. Then he put the glasses back on. Danny had to suppress a grin because Professor Graham looked a bit like Eric Morecambe.

"So you both want to come here and study English?"

Danny nodded.

"Yes," said Caroline.

Danny looked round quickly at her. She glanced back at him and winked.

"I'd like to study here," she said to the professor, "but I don't know whether to come this year or wait until after sixth year."

"Well, sometimes an extra year at school is better," said the professor. "It means you're able to cope with the work better."

"That's what I think," said Caroline.

That's what I think, too, Danny wanted to say, but he was still staring at Caroline. He felt like his mouth was gaping and he was scrambling about looking for the right question to ask her.

"My mum and dad keep talking about me going to university after fifth year, but I think it would be better to wait," she said.

"And have you told them that?"

"Not yet."

"So have you decided on this university then?" he asked.

"Yes. Well, hopefully, if I pass my exams. It's the best place to study English. That's what everyone says."

"Well, I'm glad everyone says that," said the professor. "And what about you, young man? You've been very quiet."

Danny looked round at the professor.

"Me?"

"Are you planning to come here too?"

"Well… I… Well…"

"Don't worry about him," said Caroline. "He just gets a bit tongue-tied sometimes."

Danny was blushing again. "The same as her," he muttered, immediately cringing as he heard the words out loud. The professor nodded and turned his attention back to Caroline. Danny wished the couch would open up and eat him. If only they were in a Roald Dahl book right now, then maybe that would happen. He could hear the professor talking, but he wasn't really absorbing any of the information.

His mind was in turmoil, a mixture of embarrassment and relief. The embarrassment was obvious and real, while the relief was in the fact that none of his friends had witnessed his humiliation. After another few minutes, which seemed to Danny like the longest he'd ever experienced, Professor Graham stood up, which was the signal for Caroline and Danny to do so too.

"Well, I hope to see you here at some point in the future," he said.

"Me too," Caroline said.

Danny nodded and then led the way out the office, since he was nearest the door. He began walking down the corridor at a quicker pace now, desperate to get out of the building.

"What's the hurry," Caroline said, almost breaking into a jog to keep up with him.

Danny shrugged.

"Come on, don't be like that," she said, touching his arm.

Danny stopped. "I thought you were here."

"What?"

"A student. I thought you were a student." What was wrong with him today? He'd suddenly lost the ability to speak in coherent sentences.

"No, I'm still at school."

"But you knew where you were going."

"I asked someone downstairs after wandering about lost for ten minutes."

"And your clothes."

"What about my clothes?"

"You look like a student."

Caroline glanced up and down at herself, and then shrugged.

"Did you not have to wear your uniform?"

"We did, but I brought other stuff with me to change into. I didn't want to walk about looking like a schoolgirl."

Now it was Danny who checked himself over.

"Nice blazer," said Caroline.

"Thanks," said Danny, managing to conjure up a tiny grin. There was nothing else he could do.

"Saint Angela's?"

"Yes. How do you know?"

"It says so on the badge," she said, nodding towards the blazer.

Danny automatically touched the breast pocket that had the school badge sewn on it, which included the motto 'Educatio est solum possibile per amorem.' It was the motto of Saint Angela, the patron saint of the school. Translated, it read 'Education is only possible through love.' Danny decided not to mention that to Caroline. He was sure she'd poke fun at that too.

They reached the stairs and stopped. It was up another floor up for the contemporary European literature class. Danny was eager to head down and out into the fresh air.

"I'm at West Park," Caroline said.

"West Park Secondary?"

Caroline nodded.

"Really?"

"Why would I make that up?"

"West Park Secondary?" Danny said again.

Caroline opened her bag, rummaging about and then pulling something out. She held it up. It was the West Park Secondary tie. He recognised it immediately. It was black with red pin-stripes running through it. She stuffed it back into the bag which she then slung over her shoulder again.

"What's wrong? Cat got your tongue?" she said.

"Why didn't you say you went to West Park?"

"You never asked."

"I just presumed..." He didn't bother finishing the sentence. He had been foolish enough for one day.

"So are you just here on your own?" Caroline asked.

"No, the school ran a bus."

"Is no-one else interested in doing English then?"

"I don't know. A couple of my pals are away to the Russian Department."

"The Russian Department?"

"I know."

"Do they want to study Russian?"

"Apparently you get free iced-tea if you go there."

Caroline started laughing.

"Seriously. That's where they are now."

"Maybe that's where everyone from my school went too. I haven't seen anyone else since I got here."

"I don't think my pals are planning on coming

here anyway," said Danny. "So are you going to wait until next year to come here?"

"I hope so. I still need to convince my mum and dad, and pass Higher English, of course."

"I know what you mean. My mum's desperate for me to go this year. It's all she talks about."

"Mine too. I think it's because I'd be the first in the family to go to university. But a year wouldn't make a difference."

"My sister's already here, so it's just expected that I'll go too."

"Do you not want to?"

"No, I do. I just don't think I'm ready. I mean, I was barely even able to speak in there." He shook his head. Caroline laughed. Danny smiled.

"Maybe you should tell my parents I don't want to go this year and I'll tell yours," she said. "It would be like that Hitchcock film, you know the one where they swap murders."

"Strangers on a Train."

"I love that film."

"Me too."

"We could swap murders."

"Metaphorically, of course."

"Of course," Caroline said.

"What about just writing anonymous letters? That might be safer in my mum's case."

"Why? Is she scary?"

"Scary? No." Danny laughed. His mum was anything but scary, but she was set in her ways. She was also a Catholic and Caroline was not, but he didn't mention that. "She just thinks she always knows best," he said.

"I know what you mean."

"Maybe we should just pluck up the courage and tell them face-to-face."

"Maybe. So I'll see you this September then?"

They both started laughing.

"I hope not," said Danny.

"Thanks very much."

"You know what I mean."

They both stood in silence and it felt to Danny that it was the first time Caroline had stopped talking since she'd walked up the stairs. She started rummaging in her bag again and Danny glanced at his watch. They were all to meet at half past two to get the bus back to school, so he had just over half an hour to kill before then.

"I think I'm going to go and find my Russian friends," he said.

"Are you not going up to any other classes?" Caroline said, closing her bag over.

"No, I think I'll quit while I'm behind."

Caroline smiled. "Well, it was nice to meet you, Danny Dickens."

"You too," he said. "And I'll see you here in September."

"Nineteen eighty-two."

"Hopefully."

Danny started walking downstairs, his footsteps as loud as before. He didn't dare look back, even though he wanted to. He didn't want to risk Caroline catching him looking round. That would just be the final embarrassment.

The record shop was still open. He could see the glow from inside like a lighthouse in the distance, but instead of warning him to steer a different and safer path, it was drawing him inexorably towards the shop. Danny quickened his step, glancing again at his watch. He had about ten minutes to spare. He would just about make it.

When he stepped into the shop, the bell above the door announced his entrance. There was one customer in the shop, a man standing at the counter who looked about the same age as Danny's dad. He glanced round at Danny and smiled nervously before turning away. The walls were plastered with album covers of every musical genre Danny could think of, while the ceiling had giant posters stuck to them. Vic, the shop owner, appeared from the stock room behind the cash-till, waving an album triumphantly in the air.

"I knew we had a copy," he said to the older guy. Danny couldn't see what the record was.

Vic seemed to run the shop on his own most of the time, except on a Saturday when a younger guy called Smithy helped out. Vic was older even than the customer in the shop just now, though Danny and his pals could never guess his age. They'd asked him once. "You're only as old as who you feel," he'd replied with a grin. None of them knew what that meant. Vic had long silver hair tied permanently in a pony-tail, while his face was alternatively clean shaven or bearded. The pony-tail would normally have been considered a bit girly, but on Vic it seemed like the right look. He wore denims that were so faded to be almost white, and a selection of tour t-shirts, anything from Iron Maiden to Abba.

They had made a few cranks phone-calls to the shop after the Department S single came out. "Is Vic there?" one of them would say, barely able to suppress the laughter.

"This is Vic," the voice at the other end of the phone would reply.

"Is Vic there?"

"This is Vic. Who's this?"

"Is Vic there?" They would all sing the line from the song and Vic would slam the phone down. They'd done it a few times, and Danny was sure they weren't the only ones.

The man bought his record and quickly exited the shop, probably sighing with relief when he stepped into the fresh air. Danny shuffled up to the counter.

"Alright, my man," Vic said. "What brings you here at this hour? It's almost closing time."

"Do you have the Duran Duran single?"

"Planet Earth?"

Danny nodded.

"I most certainly do." Vic plucked a seven-inch record from a shelf behind him, instinctively knowing where to locate it. "That will be seventy-five of Her Majesty's pennies, please," he said.

Danny took out a handful of coins from his pocket and rummaged through them, picking out seven ten-pence pieces, four one-pences and two half-pence coins, which he handed over to Vic.

"Did you raid someone's piggy-bank?"

"Paper money," said Danny, picking up the record.

"Do you want a bag for it?"

"Please."

Vic produced a small white plastic bag from under the counter. On it was printed, in black lettering, 'Vinyl Countdown', with the letter 'O' in

'Countdown' replaced both times by the image of a record. Danny had a few of those, along with the bigger, album-sized ones, lying in his bedroom. Vic held the bag open and Danny slipped the single inside.

"Thanks," he said, taking the bag.

The shop bell rang and Vic looked up as Danny glanced round. He turned away and then immediately turned back again. It was the girl from university. Caroline. She looked different. For one thing, she had her school uniform on, the West Park tie visible beneath her coat which was unzipped. She wore a plain white blouse and black skirt which was longer than the denim one she had on earlier in the week. Gone, too, were the Doc Martins, replaced by plain black shoes with a small heel. She wasn't wearing thick, black tights either.

"Still staring at me, I see" she said. "Are you sure you don't want me to send you a picture and that way you can look at me even when I'm not there?"

"No, I'm fine."

"Do you two know each other?" Vic asked.

"Yes," said Caroline.

"No," said Danny.

"He's been following me about since we met at university."

"No, I haven't," Danny said.

"I thought you were both still at school?"

"It was an open day at the university," Danny said.

"And just three days later, we meet again. Are you sure you're not following me?"

Danny shook his head and Caroline leant on the counter as Vic disappeared into the stock room.

"What have you got there?" she asked.

"Just a record."

"You're kidding? A record? I thought it was a football. Who is it?"

"Duran Duran. It's their debut single."

"Duran Duran? You mean, that weird band who were on Top of the Pops last week."

Danny nodded.

"Lipstick and frilly shirts and all that." Caroline made a face. "You don't like them, do you?"

"The song's good."

"What's it called again?"

"Planet Earth."

"Planet Earth. So you like boys who wear make-up then?"

"No."

"I just thought since you like Duran Duran."

"I like the song."

"Do you wear make-up?"

"No."

"Let me see."

She moved closer to him, staring at his face and he stumbled back. Music suddenly came on in the shop and Caroline stopped. She shook her head and turned round, arms folded, and faced the stock-room door through which Vic re-appeared.

"Very funny," she said as Vic grinned.

Danny didn't understand what was going on, although when the chorus of the song arrived and Vic started singing, swaying to the left and right with his arms aloft like he was holding an invisible scarf, he had to smile. "Sweet Caroline.... Good times never seem so good..."

"Turn that off," Caroline said, though she was smiling as she said it.

"So that's your song then?" Danny asked as Vic disappeared again, the music fading within a few seconds.

"Vic seems to think it's funny to play it every time I come in here."

"Well, it is quite funny."

"I don't think so. What would your song be then, Danny Dickens?"

"I don't have one."

He didn't want to tell her that Danny Boy was his song and had been for as long as he could remember. He always sang it at family parties, even now, though he did so under protest. His mum had taught him the song when he was younger, barely at primary school, and then he would perform it in front of all his aunts and uncles and cousins, standing in the middle of the room and singing in a high-pitched voice. He'd enjoyed being the centre of attention, but that had been a long, long time ago.

"Right, I need to close up," Vic said, glancing at his watch as he re-emerged into the shop. "Do you want your record then? I've kept one aside for you."

He picked out a record from one of the shelves and put it on the counter. It was the Duran Duran single, the same one that Danny had just bought. He stared at the cover and then at Caroline.

"I like boys who wear make-up," she said, winking at him. Caroline gave Vic a one-pound note, waiting with her hand outstretched until he dropped the change into her palm. He put her record into a bag without asking and then, with the two of them now carrying identical bags, they left with Vic at their heels to lock the door as soon as they were outside. He gave them a short salute before turning and heading back to the counter. Danny and Caroline both stood on the pavement, continuing to stare into the shop like they were watching a cinema screen.

"I guess we might be listening to the same record tonight," Caroline said after a few moments.

"You mean that weird band who were on Top of the Pops last week?"

Caroline laughed. "At least I know you might actually have some taste in music."

"I like Joy Division," Danny said, remembering the badge on Caroline's biker jacket.

"I'm impressed," she said. "First or second album?"

"Definitely the first."

"Really?"

He nodded. He didn't want to admit he'd only heard snatches of the second album drifting down from Frances's bedroom. He would have to plead with his sister to let him borrow it so he could tape it.

"I can't decide," said Caroline. "I think they're both brilliant. It's really sad what happened to Ian Curtis, wasn't it?"

"Love Will Tear Us Apart is one of my favourite songs," he said.

"Mine too. Maybe we've got an identical record collection?"

"I doubt it," said Danny. "Have you got Leo Sayer's greatest hits in your room?"

"Leo Sayer? You like Leo Sayer? Oh my God."

"I used to like him," he said, shaking his head. "When I was a wee boy."

"What, like last week?"

"I found it lying amongst my records the other night. I couldn't believe it. What a red neck."

"Did you smash it up then?"

"No, I just put it back in with my dad's records."

"I think I'd die if I found that in my room," Caroline said. "I'm trying to think if I've got anything embarrassing in my collection. I have a funny feeling there's a Boney M album lurking about somewhere."

"You're kidding?"

"No."

"That's got to be worse than Leo Sayer?"

"I don't know. They're probably both as bad as each other."

"Let's never speak of this again," Caroline said. "Deal?"

Danny shook her hand which she held out to him.

"So where do you stay then?" she asked.

"Foresthill Drive."

"That's not far from me. I'm in Park Avenue. Are you heading home?"

Danny nodded.

"Maybe I'll join you then."

Danny's house was only about ten minutes from the centre of the town, while Park Avenue was only another five minutes further on. Danny felt his pace slowed with every stride he took, like he was trying to drag out the time until they would head in different directions. Danny told her about his three sisters. Frances had a 'cool taste in music', Theresa was a 'typical annoying nine-year-old', and Marie, who was a year younger than him, was just 'annoying'.

Caroline told him about her brother. His name was Graeme. They were twins. "He is really annoying," she said. "We don't have anything in common, so we don't really have much to do with each other."

Her favourite subject at school was English. He already guessed that. Her favourite book that she told people about was Catcher in the Rye. "I know everyone says that," she said. Her favourite book that she didn't usually admit to was Watership Down.

"The one about the rabbits?" Danny asked.

"Yes. Have you read it?"

"No, but I've seen the film."

"I love the film too. I've seen it like a hundred times. I know it's not cool or trendy or anything like that, but I love it, almost as much as the book."

"As long as you don't start singing Bright Eyes."

"Don't worry, I won't."

He told her about his favourite books. Catch 22 and Catcher in the Rye. "And To Kill A Mockingbird too," he added.

They argued about their favourite Roald Dahl book. "It's got to be Charlie and the Chocolate Factory," Danny said, although Caroline preferred The Twits. They had both read Enid Blyton when they were younger.

"I used to think the Secret Seven were the coolest people in the world," said Danny, "and I thought it would be great to be a member until I got old enough to realise I'd be joining the SS. Then I went off them."

"Probably just as well."

They talked more about music and television and films. He even admitted that he always felt sad whenever he watched *Von Ryan's Express*.

"I've never seen it," she said.

"Frank Sinatra plays this American prisoner during the war, and he leads an escape. They're trying to catch a train which will take them through a tunnel into Switzerland and the Germans are chasing them, and Frank Sinatra's the last one to get on the train, and he's almost there when the Germans shoot him. And he dies on the track as the rest of the prisoners on the train escape. It's so sad."

He stopped talking, aware that Caroline was grinning.

"What's so funny?"

"You are."

"Me? Why, what have I done?"

"It's a film about soldiers and you make it sound like the saddest film in the world."

"No, I don't."

"I think it's cute that it makes you so sad."

"Cute?" Danny almost spat the word out, it tasted so disgusting in his mouth.

"Okay then. Sweet."

"Sweet? As in sweet Caroline…?"

He sang the words although he knew the tune bore no resemblance to the song Vic had played earlier on in the shop. Caroline laughed and pushed him away gently.

"I hate that song," she said.

"I don't even know who sings it but it's now my new favourite song."

"It's Neil Diamond. My dad always sings it at family parties after he's had a few drinks. It's so embarrassing."

Danny almost told her about his Danny Boy performances but something held him back from revealing it. It was enough that he'd told her about Leo Sayer.

"I'll need to go," Caroline said, looking beyond Danny. He glanced round and saw two boys walking along the street towards them. "It's just a couple of my brother's pals," she said, noticing his puzzled look.

"Is it too embarrassing to be seen talking to me in public?" he asked.

"No, it's not that. It's just… Look, I've got to go. It's been nice talking to you again, Danny Dickens. Enjoy your Duran Duran record," she said, crossing the road and heading towards Park Avenue. This time he did watch her as she quickly walked away, getting smaller and smaller with every stride.

"It was nice talking to you too," he muttered.

This is an extract from Paul Cuddihy's forthcoming novel, 66 Days.

Of Crime And Passion

Mitigating circumstances. That's what they'd say. Poor little deaf kid, they'd think, with expressions of pity and patronising words no-one believed he'd understand, but he did. It made him smile when he thought about it. The reaction was so predictable. He could already picture it, where everyone would be placed in the room, in orbit around his own body sitting centre-stage, head bowed, full of remorse but secretly laughing at the whole situation. Sorry? Not a chance.

He had planned this operation meticulously, thinking of nothing else for weeks but the details of the task ahead. Truth be told, however, it wasn't an intricate plan, but simple in its execution, with little chance of detection or error. The repercussions he already anticipated, though he hoped they wouldn't be too severe. Anyway, it would be a price worth paying.

He glanced at his watch. Only fifteen more minutes before he needed to set out. A sudden knot twisted sharply in his stomach but it was strangely comforting. Nerves would keep him focused and on edge.

"What are you doing today?" his mum asked, signing the words with her hands to accompany her voice, though he could more or less deduce, from the movement of her lips, what she was saying. A useful skill, it enabled him to eavesdrop when people presumed he was out of the loop.

"I'm going into town," he signed to her.

"Who with?"

"Myself."

"Do you want any company? I'm not doing anything."

"No, it's fine. I'll not be in for long."

"What are you going into town for?"

He hesitated before replying, his hands poised, ready to communicate whatever white lie he opted to tell him mum. He wondered what she'd say if he just blurted it out now. Probably think he was joking. He smiled.

"What's so funny?" she asked.

"Nothing," he signed, shaking his head to wipe the grin from his face. "I'm just going window shopping," he explained, smiling again at his own, unintentional joke.

"What is so funny, Liam?" his mum asked, her face displaying a mixture of puzzlement and irritation that transmitted itself to her hands, which signed with an increased degree of frustration. She shook her head when he remained silent.

"Teenagers," she said, not bothering to gesture with her hands this time. He shrugged his shoulders as she shook her head again and walked out of the room. He glanced at his watch. Time to go.

It was just as well he'd checked when the bus would arrive. It was a horrible day. Rain was falling heavily and the wind battered and buffeted it in every direction, mainly, or so it seemed to Liam, right into his chilled face. He pulled his woolly hat further down over his ears as he stepped on to the bus.

The driver stared at him impatiently as he held out the palm of his hand to display the one pound coin and tiny silver five pence for his fare. He put the money into the machine and gestured 'ONE' with his index finger. The driver looked puzzled so Liam did it again, pointing to the money in the machine as well. Suddenly the driver's face changed, as if a light had just been turned on inside his brain.

"You – want – a – ticket – into – town," he said with exaggerated slowness.

"I'm not a fuckin' moron, you fuckin' arsehole," Liam signed, while smiling at the same time.

The driver smiled and nodded, pointing at the machine where Liam's ticket had appeared. He gave Liam the thumbs-up sign as he grabbed the ticket without further reply, waiting until Liam sat down before moving off from the bus stop.

Liam was glad to take the weight off his feet and, more importantly, the rucksack off his shoulders. He could feel the pain stretching across the top of his back as he manoeuvred it on to the floor at his feet. It was heavy. He wondered if his dad would notice the missing boulder from the small rockery in the back garden that was his pride and joy. He'd know soon enough who the culprit was and for what purpose it had been used.

The rain fell with the same relentless rhythm when he arrived in the city centre. Glasgow's streets were coated with a shiny black veneer while the sky was grey as far as the eye could see.

The bus stop was just round the corner from the music shop and Liam, almost trailing the rucksack along the floor, got off the bus without glancing at the driver. He heaved the bag on to his shoulders again and began walking purposefully towards the shop, his stomach once more jangling with nerves. It was nearly time and he was anxious to begin.

He stopped in front of the shop window, removed

the rucksack, placing it on the wet pavement, and stared through the glass. Taking centre-stage in its full glory and splendour was the object of his affection and the reason for his mission. The drum kit seemed to beckon him, calling out through the plate glass barrier that separated them. He glanced up and down the street. It was almost deserted save for a few hardy souls who'd sacrificed their Sunday afternoon to battle the elements. Perfect.

He had always loved drums. For as long as he could remember they held a particular fascination, though it was difficult to explain and impossible for others to understand. When he was barely two-years-old, he'd toddled into the kitchen behind his mum, and while she busied herself at the sink he had opened one of the cupboards and proceeded to empty its contents on to the cold, tiled floor.

It was the stainless steel pots which aroused his curiosity; they became helmets which covered his hair and slipped down over the top of his eyes, leaving him in temporary darkness. That game quickly lost its appeal and the helmets became drums. Turned upside down he used his fingers to hit the bottom of the pots before he discovered a potato peeler previously dropped on the floor and began using that to bang the pots. Almost immediately, the peeler was snatched out of his hand and he found himself lifted off the floor and spirited back into the living room to be given his toy train as amusement, but in those few seconds he had felt something as he banged the pots, a vibration up his arm that was both thrilling and unsettling, a feeling that never ceased to excite him even as he got older and pots and cardboard boxes were thrashed with vigorous intensity.

He had always craved his own kit, had coveted one after seeing a picture in his mum's catalogue but Santa remained deaf to his pleas.

It was love at first sight when he saw the spotlit kit in the window of the Helter Skelter Music Store. He had stopped abruptly and ventured right up to the window, pressing his face against the glass like a hungry man outside a restaurant. This was what he wanted, had always wanted but knew was a hopeless dream. His parents couldn't grasp his need and he couldn't articulate it. The music store, he knew, would be no better and he'd probably be laughed out of the shop. A deaf boy wanting to try out a £1,500 drum kit. Not a chance.

So as far as Liam was concerned, he had no other choice. He could wait several years before he'd saved up enough money to buy the kit but he'd never be able to wait that long. He had to play these drums … now.

He crouched down and unzipped the rucksack, first slipping on his mum's gardening gloves. Next he removed the sticks he'd bought at Helter Skelter last week, putting them into the inside pocket of his jacket. Then he gripped the large, dirt-covered boulder and stood, adjusting it in his hands to make sure he'd get an accurate and powerful throw. Taking one last look around, he stepped back to the edge of the pavement, took a deep breath and sprang forward, launching the boulder at the glass when he was just a few feet from it.

The boulder burst through the glass, leaving a gaping hole but, more importantly, shattering a large portion of the window. Liam didn't stop to admire his handiwork but immediately stepped forward and aimed a powerful kick at the weakened window, sending more of its small particles into the shop display and out on to the pavement. Another couple of well-placed kicks and there was a big enough gap for him to squeeze inside.

Liam quickly sat down behind the drum kit, removing the gloves and stuffing them into his jacket pocket before bringing out the drumsticks. He could feel his face breaking out into a wide grin as he fingered the sticks, letting them roll back and forth in the sweaty palm of his hand.

He hit one of the golden symbols gently, watching it vibrate for a few moments. He nodded approvingly and brought the sticks crashing down, closing his eyes and instinctively finding each drum, feeling the vibrations shimmer up his arms.

Opening his eyes, still grinning, Liam was aware he was now playing in front of an audience. A young couple, the girl with her arm linked into her boyfriend's, standing amidst the fragments of glass strewn across the pavement, watched his musical exertions with amusement. Behind them, a car had stopped in the middle of the road, its occupants staring at Liam like they were at a safari park studying one of the animals from the safety of their vehicle. The two little girls in the back were pointing urgently towards the broken window and the boy sitting playing the drums, their mouths moving silently behind their own glass barrier.

The perplexed, almost awe-struck gazes that never left him only forced Liam to play with even greater energy and urgency. He closed his eyes again, savouring each and every moment of his very own golden silence.

Careless Memories

I once asked dad his proudest moment. Quick as a flash he replied, "Italy winning the 1982 World Cup."

Never mind the birth of his four children, his wedding day or the moment he first set eyes on mum – fifteen years of flaming hair hiding behind her parents, avoiding eye-contact with the boy who set her heart racing. It was love at first sight that summer's day on the seafront at Ayr.

"July the fifteenth, nineteen forty-eight," mum would say whenever we asked her to recount the story. Dad sat in the armchair that was his and his alone, shaking his head, but we saw the sparkle in his eyes when he looked at mum, or whispered sweet nothings in his smoky-breathed Italian accent when he thought no-one was watching. He loved his Eileen with as much passion and intensity as when he first set eyes on her, a schoolgirl on holiday with her family, him a young man of twenty-one, selling soothing ice-cream for parched throats.

They never spoke that first time. Mum just nodded when asked if she'd like a cone. But dad sought her out, appearing at the beach or in the expanse of grass behind the seafront where mum and Aunt Margaret played with a ball, or even at their table one night as they sat eating fish suppers in a cafe.

Francisco Renucci – "Everyone calls me Franco," he told her in between throwing the ball to her or Margaret. He'd join them when his ice-cream sold out rather than return to his father's shop for fresh supplies, which would later earn him a clip round the ear and a volley of abuse in machine-gun Italian. There were no objections from either girl. Who wouldn't want to be seen playing with the boy whose looks had caught the attention of many other girls along the promenade? But Margaret was only twelve and while she might have harboured a crush for Franco, he only had eyes for mum.

Her age was a major stumbling block, as was the age gap when that was discovered, and it took a combination of arguments sparked by her fiery, Irish temper that took an eternity to rouse but was a tempest in full flow, and dad's persistence – travelling up from Ayr to the south side of Glasgow every weekend for chaperoned dates – which eventually wore down my grandparents' objections. Just under two years after that first encounter at the seaside, my mum, having turned seventeen a fortnight before, walked down the aisle of St John's Church in the Gorbals on the arm of her father. Aunt Margaret followed behind, clutching a feeble bouquet of flowers, while my grandmother sobbed quietly in the front row, oblivious to the occasional frowns from Father O'Hara standing at the foot of the altar waiting for the bride-to-be to reach the handsome young man standing proudly in the freshly pressed black suit he'd borrowed from a cousin. The church has long since vanished, erased like so much of the past, along with the street it once stood on.

My favourite picture of my parents is a black and white image taken outside the church – the newly-married Mr and Mrs Renucci. She's wearing a nervous smile, perhaps with thoughts of her impending wedding night weighing heavily on her mind, while he grins, probably with slightly different thoughts of the impending wedding night. I got the photograph blown up and framed for their thirtieth wedding anniversary and it continues to hang proudly in their living room, a time of innocence caught forever on camera. I wonder if dad, when he used to look at it, remembered the day or recognised the young couple in the frame.

There are many things he no longer remembers. Our names. Who we are. Where he is. Mum makes a daily pilgrimage to the care home he now stays in, praying for a rare moment of recognition but knowing he will greet her like a stranger. I prefer to go myself. Mum's pain and dad's bewilderment is often too hard to witness.

We sit and talk. Well, I talk and he stares into space. On sunny days I dress him in his warmest clothes and we wander outside and park ourselves on one of the wooden benches planted in the middle of the garden. I don't know if the fresh air does him any good, but there are times when we almost have a conversation. The weather. Birds singing in the trees. The state of the garden. It's not much but it means everything to me. I fill the inevitable silences with my own memories, which seem to grow more vivid as his fade from view.

"Remember when Italy won the World Cup? Remember that, dad?"

Of course he doesn't. Proudest moment of his life. Once he would talk about it with the enthusiasm of a small child describing the presents Santa had brought, and I would hang on to every word. I remember it myself, the house a sea of bodies like someone was bidding to make the Guinness Book of Records for the most people crammed into a semi-detached, three-bedroom house, everyone wearing the sparkling blue of the Azzurri or the red, white and green of the Italian flag. I had draped one flag out of my bedroom window, eager to let everyone know where our loyalties lay.

Dad, the self-appointed cheerleader, wandered from room to room, re-filling glasses of wine, handing out cans of Tennent's lager, breaking into chants of 'Italia! Italia!' at every opportunity. We were split between living room and dining room, with a television in each, all eyes glued to the screen, a collective prayer rising up for an Italian victory.

And when Marco Tardelli scored the third goal, the goal that would bring the World Cup back to Rome, there was cheering, screaming, people jumping and hugging like a sudden storm of flesh, wave after wave rising and falling with joy. Dad stood amidst this tempest as bodies bumped into him, seemingly oblivious to the chaos. I was hugging my sister, Maria, the two of us screaming in unison and jumping up and down, but I could see dad, not moving or shouting or celebrating. He was crying. Tears streamed down his face and he made no effort to wipe them away. For a fleeting moment I was alarmed but almost instantly I realised they were tears of joy. Mum saw him too and she glided over to him, reaching up and brushing away a tear from his cheek. He moved towards her hand and kissed it gently. It was the most beautiful thing I had ever seen.

Then Alzheimer's came along, messing up the files in his mind, mixing the index cards so that he could no longer organise his daily life. The magic of that moment, when his beloved mother country brought tears to his eyes, was gone, turned to dust like the pages of an ancient manuscript touched by rough hands. Just another sadness to add to the pile already accumulated these past two years. No matter how often I talk about it, describing the goals like a football commentator, recalling the ecstasy of Tardelli's face as he ran to the touchline, there's not even the faintest flicker of recognition.

We're sitting in the television room one day, dad in the armchair directly facing the screen while I slouch on the couch, flicking through an old copy of *Hello*, only vaguely aware of the droning noise in the background.

"Forza Italia," my dad says in a weak voice. I sit up, startled, letting the magazine fall to the floor.

"What did you say? Dad? … Dad?"

He continues to stare at the television and I notice for the first time the blue shirts darting about on the screen. It's a football game, Portsmouth against Grimsby Town. His pupils dance excitedly like bees in a jam jar as he follows the players chasing the ball. I've not seen him so alert for a long time. Grimsby in black and white stripes, Portsmouth in the blue of Italy.

"Forza Italia," my dad says again. His hands grip the arms of his chair so tightly I can see the veins sticking out.

"Dad, it's not Italy," I say. He doesn't hear me. I watch him for a few minutes. It's almost like he's back, good as new, eyes glued to the television, shouting for Italy. I know it can't last, and it doesn't. A break in the action for adverts is like a light switch being flicked off and he is once more sitting in darkness.

I order the DVD that night. I don't tell anyone. Not mum or my sisters, not even Kate, though I'm tempted as we lie in bed. I don't because it's my secret. Mine and dad's.

He's already sitting in the television room when Helen, one of the care workers, shows me into the room.

"Franco, you've got a visitor. It's Paolo. Your son."

Dad turns towards the door, looking directly at Helen for a moment before turning back to the television.

"We'll be fine," I say, shuffling past her and making for the television.

"Just give me a shout if you need anything," she says before disappearing out the room, closing the door behind her.

"Hi, dad." I lightly kiss his forehead and then kneel down in front of the television. He watches me, his head bobbing up and down slightly. A trail of saliva hangs out the side of his mouth and I stop to wipe it clean with a tissue.

I remove the contents of the bag – a DVD, a large Italian flag and a box of drawing pins. I unravel the flag and began pinning it on the wall behind the television. Dad's eyes flicker between the screen and me, though whether it is the flag or the blue Italian football top I'm wearing which catches his attention I don't know, but I tell myself he has recognised something even if he can't explain what it is.

The flag securely attached to the wall, I take the disc out of its case and slide it into the machine. I fast-forwarded through the copyright warnings and adverts for other DVDs until the main feature is about to start. I pause the film and 'The 1982 World Cup Final' hovers on screen in gold lettering against a black background. I stand up, my knees cracking as I straighten my body and look down on dad, whose gaze now rests on the flag.

What is he thinking of? Can he see his younger self running through the dirt track roads of Badolato, the town in southern Italy where he and his family lived until they emigrated to Scotland in nineteen thirty-one, as much for his father's own safety as for any dreams of making their fortune? Socialists did not tend to have a long life-span in Mussolini's Italy. Is it the barbed wire of the camp on the Isle of Man where he and his father and his brothers were interned during the Second World War? He would lightly touch the metal with his fingertips and stare at the carpet of green and yellow which stretched as far as the eye could see, dreaming of running freely through those fields until his lungs were fit to burst.

Or does he remember Sunday, July 11th, 1982, and all the people packed into our house? His friends. His family. His Eileen.

I sit down on the table beside his chair and point the remote control at the DVD machine. The television screen dances back into the life with the regal tones of a brass band announcing the main attraction. Then the Italian and West German players stride out of the tunnel into the humid Madrid night. I glance at dad but immediately look back to the screen. I want to see his reaction but I'm not sure I can bear it if there is nothing.

I wait for the goals, hoping that they will provide the catalyst for something … anything. I'm almost tempted to press fast forward.

"Foul! Dirty German bastard."

I nearly fall off the table as dad shouts at the German defender Paul Breitner, who has just fouled Roberto Bettega. I burst out laughing. Accompanying the words are the faintest traces of a hand gesture. He had always been so articulate with his hands and arms, unable to say anything without painting a picture with his limbs on an invisible canvas. The rest of the game is punctuated with occasional shouts, usually abusive and anti-German. It's more than I could have hoped for.

With eight minutes of the match remaining, Marco Tardelli scores *that* goal. I'm on my feet cheering, the emotion of the occasion in the television room sweeping me up like a leaf caught by a sudden gust of wind while dad claps. He claps. Tears well up in my eyes and roll down my cheeks and I have a sudden, overwhelming urge to hug him. He sits, a smile on his face that I imagine he wore when he first saw mum on that Ayr seafront, and he waves his arms in front of him.

"We've won the cup, Paolo," he says and I cry. He remembered my name. He remembers.

He retains the nervous excitement of the game even after it finishes and Italy have paraded the trophy round the stadium, though I can see that it is beginning to fade. I stop the DVD and return to the start, wiping my tear-stained face with my sleeve as I wind through the adverts. Pressing the play button, I kneel at dad's side as the music begins and we wait to see if Italy will win the World Cup again.

This story was first published in The Scotsman newspaper in July 2014 under the title, Proudest Moment'.

Sound Of Thunder

Charlie's black suit hung on the door frame like a headless anorexic. There was a white stain on one of the lapels from the last time he'd worn it. Ice-cream. Alison had tried rubbing it out without much success. It was a pity it wasn't a wedding he was going to. A sprig of heather would have concealed the stain. There was nothing he could do, however. It was the only suit he owned. A freshly ironed white shirt was draped across the back of a chair with a black tie placed on top of it. Alison had done it for him. She had the ironing board up and was already pressing out the creases in the shirt before he even had time to protest at all the fuss.

"It's Cathy's funeral and I want you looking your best," she said.

He shook his head as he sat down, putting his mug of tea on top of a coaster on the glass table at the side of the chair.

"It's not like she's going to notice," he muttered.

"That's a terrible thing to say, dad. God forgive you."

Charlie shrugged but didn't say anything else. She was so like her mother, standing at the ironing board the way Isobel used to do, and giving him into trouble the way she used to do as well. Isobel had been dead ten years last February. He was well used to his own company now, but it was these sudden and unexpected glimpses of the way life used to be which reminded him how much he still missed her. Isobel would have made sure he looked smart for the funeral. Cathy was his best friend's wife. Well, his ex-best friend, actually. Isobel would have stopped that from spiralling out of control as well.

"What are you smiling about?" Alison asked.

"Nothing."

"That's your shirt done."

"I'm still not sure about going."

"You've got to go, dad. You were all such good friends."

"Exactly. We were."

"You've still got to pay your respects. That's what mum would have told you to do."

Charlie stood in the living room wearing only his boxer shorts and a pair of black socks. He took the white shirt off the chair and put it on, slowly buttoning it up. He pointed the remote control at the television and immediately *BBC News 24* came on. That's what he watched most of the time, though it was often just background noise while he read a book or tackled *The Herald* crossword. A girl on the screen was reporting from the Horn of Africa about an imminent famine which could affect ten million people. There had been famines there for as long as Charlie could remember, and no doubt there would continue to be so, long after he had taken his place alongside Isobel.

He padded through to the kitchen. All that talk of famine had made him hungry and he popped a couple of slices of bread into the toaster. He would just spread butter on them this morning. He was tempting fate if he used jam. The stain on his jacket was bad enough. He didn't want to compound it with a dark red one on his white shirt. The kettle didn't take long to boil and he poured the hot water into the tea-pot, watching the solitary bag swirling in the hot liquid which slowly turned the shade of rust.

It would be lunch-time before he returned home, and he'd be starving by then if he didn't eat now. Usually that wasn't a problem since he'd head to wherever the post-funeral meal was being served, but not today. Today he was coming straight back home. Funerals were part of his life now. That was the inevitability of growing old. People died, but not just people. Wives. Brothers. Sisters. Cousins. Friends. Friends' wives... ex-friend's wives. One day soon it would be his turn. He always liked funeral food as well. It was usually steak pie and potatoes. It was almost tempting enough to swallow his pride and attend. Almost.

It wasn't funeral weather. The sky was a perfect, unblemished sheet of blue, and Charlie could feel beads of sweat running down his back as he drove towards the church. Saint Michael's was where he'd grown up, serving as an altar boy, his mother speculating that was him on the first rung of the ladder towards priesthood. First Communion. Confirmation. He and Isobel had got married there. Children were baptised. Parents buried. Isabel too. It had been the same for Paddy. The two of them had been friends since primary school, and their lives had seemed to run in comfortable parallel.

He imagined they would grow old together. When Isobel died, Paddy and Cathy had been a great source of strength and support. He should have been able to reciprocate now. After all, he knew exactly what Paddy was going through, but Paddy was on his own with this. There had been no phone-call from Paddy or from any of his children. Why would they when he and their dad hadn't spoken for over a year now? It was Frank Lafferty, one of the parishioners at Saint Michael's, who'd called him. "I just thought you should know," Frank said.

Charlie parked his car in a side street about fifty yards from the church. He didn't want to use the car park. People would see him and he'd know they were whispering about what had happened. He knew they still did, whenever anyone spotted him at church or the shops or the bookies. They would only see him outside that place now. He couldn't set foot in it again, not after everything that had happened.

It had been a sunny day like today when he'd phoned Paddy.

"I'm not going to make it today," he had said. "I've got Alison's kids. She's on a course, something to do with work."

"We can leave it 'til next week if you want," Paddy said. "It's not like there's anything big on today."

"Sound of Thunder in the two-thirty at Newcastle," Charlie said as he glanced at the betting page in the *Daily Record*. He often wondered later how different life would have been if he hadn't said anything. He and Paddy met every Wednesday at the bookies. They would place a few bets, pop next door to Donnelly's for a pint in between races, and then saunter back to watch another horse fail to win.

"What are the odds?" Paddy asked.

"Thirty-three to one."

"Thirty-three to one!"

"I know, but I've got a good feeling about it, Paddy."

"A good feeling?"

"I think the odds are too high. It's done okay in its last two races, and it runs better when the ground's a bit soft."

"But thirty-three to one, Charlie."

"Just put a couple of quid on it."

"I don't know, Charlie. I might not bother going if you'll not be there."

"No problem, but if you do, it's Sound of Thunder."

"I know. Two-thirty at Newcastle."

They always had a twenty-pound kitty. They'd bet a pound here, a couple of pounds there, sometimes on the nose but usually it was each-way bets. Less risk that way, more chance of winning a few pounds, and anyway, it wasn't about the money. Whatever they did win was usually spent in the pub or split fifty-fifty if one of them – usually Paddy – had to go home. Charlie only had an empty house waiting for him so he was never in any hurry to leave. More often than not, the two of them, slightly worse for wear, would end up in Paddy's house, scoffing down whatever Cathy served up to them while she gently scolded them for being a couple of drunken old fools.

Charlie could see people walking into church, men in dark suits, white shirts and black ties, women in a variety of black outfits, younger ones wearing skirts that were suitably sombre in colour if less appropriate in length. He opened the car door and got out, standing beside the vehicle after locking it. He would sit at the back of the church where he was less likely to be noticed. He didn't want to look any of them in the eye today. What would they say to him? What could he say to them? At least he'd be here. They wouldn't be able to say anything about that. He was doing the right thing. He was here to pay his final respects, and that was the only thing which mattered.

Still, something stopped him from moving away from the car. Maybe it would be better just to wait until everyone was inside and Mass had started so that he could slip in unnoticed and then slip away at the end before they carried Cathy out of the church, so long as they didn't spot him, like he was trying to escape or was embarrassed at being noticed.

If anyone ever asked Charlie to put a price on friendship, he would tell them. "One thousand, five hundred and ninety-one pounds and eighty-seven pence," not offering anything else by way of explanation. He would know, however, and Paddy would too. It had been Frank Lafferty who told Charlie this news too, in the frozen meat aisle of the local supermarket.

"Out spending your winnings?" Frank asked.

"Just getting a few bits and pieces," said Charlie.

"For a wee celebration, I suppose?"

Charlie looked at the packet of mince in his hand and then back at Frank.

"Celebrating what?"

"Oh, it's like that, then?" Frank said with a laugh. "You don't want any publicity after your big win?

Don't worry, your secret's safe with me."

"Sorry, Frank. You've lost me."

"Your big win yesterday at the bookies."

"I wasn't at the bookies yesterday."

"But Paddy was. He had a big win."

"Did he?"

"About sixteen hundred pounds, I think. I just presumed you knew about it."

"He must be keeping it a surprise 'til later," Charlie said. Making his excuses, he headed over to the newspapers to check the results. Sound of Thunder must have won, he thought, and Paddy had put a lot more on it than their usual twenty pounds.

He scanned the racing results page. Sound of Thunder hadn't even been placed. When he phoned Paddy, no-one answered. He tried again. Still no-one picked up. Frank must have made a mistake. It could have been someone else who'd won the money. It might have been sixteen pounds rather than sixteen hundred. Paddy would have told him right away if he'd won anything at all, never mind as much as that. In all the years of betting together, they'd never won anything near that amount. About one hundred and fifty pounds was the most they'd ever won, and that had been a long time ago. He dialled Paddy's number again. Still nothing.

Charlie was back in his car. It had been an automatic reaction as soon as he'd seen the black limousine carrying Paddy and his children draw up in front of the church. He didn't want any of them glancing over and catching sight of him. He could still see them, however, as they stood at the steps. Paddy's daughters were clinging to their father while his sons waited anxiously for him to lead the way inside. Paddy looked shell-shocked. Charlie remembered feeling that way, too, as if everything was happening at full speed around him while he moved in slow motion. It would be later, when the house was empty of well-intentioned mourners, that it would really hit home that his wife was gone.

They all disappeared inside Saint Michael's, but still Charlie sat in his car. He thought of the last time he ever spoke to Paddy after his friend had phoned him and explained what happened.

"It was just a wee Yankee," Paddy said. "I put a couple of pounds on Sound of Thunder but it was hopeless."

"I know," said Charlie.

"I was sitting reading through the paper and I picked a few horses and decided to put them on. I didn't think it would come up."

"So how much was it?"

"One thousand, five hundred and ninety-one pounds... and eighty-seven pence."

"So what's the split then?"

There was silence on the other end of the line, and Charlie knew that nothing would ever be the same again. He went to the house later that day. Cathy answered the door. She stepped aside automatically to let him in, but he shook his head. Paddy appeared at the door and stood beside his wife.

"I'll leave you to it," she said.

"No, Cathy," said Charlie. "I'd rather you heard it too. How many years have we been friends?"

Paddy shrugged.

"And how long have we been betting together?

Your money, my money. It's never mattered before. It was always our money, whether we won or lost."

"But it was my money, Charlie. I picked the horses, I put the bet on. You weren't there."

"So what?"

"So it's my winnings."

Charlie shook his head. There was no point repeating the conversation they'd already had over the telephone.

"Have a nice life, Paddy," he muttered, turning away.

"Charlie, don't be like that," Cathy said. "Come on in and have a cup of tea and we can sort this out."

Charlie kept walking down the path, head bowed, feet shuffling along the concrete slabs. He suddenly felt old. And lonely.

"Charlie!" Cathy shouted again but he didn't look back, either in anger or sadness. He was never going to look back.

He drove away that day, just as he did now, leaving Saint Michael's behind him. He knew exactly how Paddy was feeling right now. He could have been there for him, the way Paddy had been when Isobel died. He could have put an arm round his friend's shoulders and told him that the pain would never leave him but it would become tolerable, and that each day got a little better. The comfort of children and grandchildren would see to that. Instead, he was going home and there would be no words of comfort for anyone.

Girls On Film

Graham Daniels liked taking pictures. People said it was good to have a hobby and Graham agreed. It was more than a hobby, however. It was a passion, an obsession even, something that occupied most of his thoughts and dreams. Even when he was at work he was thinking of the last picture he'd taken or imagining the next one he would take. Sometimes he already had an idea in his mind. It might be a fully-formed image and it would simply be a case of him pressing the button on the camera. Other times there was the joy of stumbling upon something so breathtaking or beautiful or perfect that it would almost be criminal not to snap it. That was where the passion came in. The thrill of taking a picture in the moment and then, upon closer examination later, realising that his instinct had been correct.

The walls of his house were littered with such images. These were the special ones that merited an elevated place beyond the computer folders and discs where he kept everything else he took. These he printed out and framed. It might be the image just as he had taken it, or he'd work on it first, adjusting the various tones and shades until he was happy with it. Some people would call that cheating but he didn't care.

His favourite picture was like that. It was a winter's day, the sky grey and pregnant with snow. There had already been a light fall and more looked set to follow. He was anxious to get home before the roads became treacherous. He had just turned into the narrow road which snaked for a mile through fields and into town, when he saw it. A deer stood perfectly still in the middle of a snow-covered field. If he didn't know any better, Graham could have sworn it was a stuffed animal. He steered the car as best as he could to the side of the road, switching on the hazard lights and snatching his camera from the passenger seat. He stepped out into the cold.

Stray specks floated aimlessly in the air, stragglers from the previous fall or portents of what was to follow. Graham shivered as he stood at the fence separating field from road. He knew he would have to be quick because the deer could bolt at any second. He caught the animal in the freeze-frame of the camera and pressed the button. The deer turned round and stared at him. He pressed again. It shook its head, in disgust or disdain he didn't know, but he took another picture. The deer glanced in the other direction as Graham kept snapping before it slowly sauntered across the field towards a cluster of anorexic trees and bushes at the far corner.

He chose the best three – the first three – and framed them as a sequence of images, making the background monochrome while the beast, which looked even more beautiful than in reality, remained resplendent in full colour. He called the picture, 'Yes, Deer.'

"That's quite funny for you," Maureen said.

She liked it too, and didn't protest when he suggested it should be hung in the living-room. It remained there even now, just above the fireplace. She often called the pictures 'his children.' She didn't mean anything by it. He knew that and he realised it was only to him that she could say such things. They never had children of their own.

It wasn't that they didn't want any. They had tried unsuccessfully for many years. There had been miscarriages, each one more heartbreaking than the last. He had wanted to stop. Maureen wanted to keep going. Eventually, they met in the middle. He was ready to continue if that's what she wanted. She accepted, painfully and reluctantly, that she was never going to have a baby.

Graham knew something like this broke many marriages, but theirs was for better or for worse, and walking away had never been an option for either of them. He had his 'children'. She had… well, she had him, and he hoped that was still enough for her.

It was a sunny day when it happened, one of those rare Saturdays in May when the sky was so blue and cloudless it felt like you could stare all the way to heaven. People sensed it and got up earlier than normal, eager to savour every moment of the sunshine. Plans were hastily made for trips to the seaside, not realising that countless others would be doing the same thing and they'd all spend far too long trapped in warm cars, and stuck in traffic jams. Barbeques were organised and visits made to the supermarket for food and drink, while store managers quickly stacked up bags of charcoal and boxes of cut-price beer at the front door to entice shoppers. Some people still remained in bed, oblivious to the sunshine. They would regret it later.

Graham and Maureen decided not to venture too far from home; a day in the garden, reading the paper or a book in between dozing on a sun lounger, or pottering about with the flowers and plants surrounding the grass. Graham had two new plants in the boot of his car that were earmarked for the bottom of the garden and he was on his way back home.

Then he saw it. In his photographer's mind, it was already perfectly framed. He immediately parked the car and almost in the same moment as he killed the engine, he snatched up his camera and was out of the car.

A water hydrant had burst. More likely, it had been deliberately broken, and it was spraying water into the air. A pool had gathered at the side of the road, and the steady stream of water shooting towards the sky showed no sign of abating. A group of children – about five or six of them – danced round the water excitedly like they were worshipping some strange cultish statue that had come alive. Then, prompted by an invisible signal, they would run through the water, screaming loudly as they were soaked. T-shirts clung heavily to their bodies, while two of the girls wore swimsuits. A wary dog hovering at the edge of the water barked nervously at the spray but did not venture into it, despite being encouraged to do so by the children.

Graham crouched down on one knee on the opposite pavement and studied the image through the lens. The sunlight shimmering through the water produced a kaleidoscope of colours and he snapped it quickly, anxious in case that moment disappeared forever, but it was still there even after he took the picture and he snapped again.

He heard the excited screams of the children and

the two swim-suited girls suddenly appeared in the shot, racing through the water. He pressed the button and caught them in the middle of the shower. He snapped their quick journey to 'dry land' – four pictures in total – and then studied the sequence on the camera. The pictures were stunning. If they were his daughters, he would definitely have printed the images and framed them.

He stood up and switched off his camera as he walked over to his car. The best pictures were always like that – sudden, unexpected moments caught forever. Maureen would like those pictures, he thought as he got in the car and put the camera back on the passenger seat.

A sudden slam against his door startled him and he dropped his keys on the floor. Another blow rattled his window.

"What are you doing?"

He glanced up at an angry red face pressed against the glass and immediately shrunk back in his seat.

"Were you taking pictures of my wee girl?"

Graham shook his head, moving even further into his car. He wished the door was locked.

"Aye you were. I saw you. Get out the car, you pervert."

The man grabbed the door handle and opened it. Graham tried to pull it shut but the man was too strong and yanked it open.

"Get out the car!"

"I haven't done anything."

The man leant in and grabbed Graham by the neck, starting to pull him out.

"Get off me," Graham shouted, trying to release the man's grip which was beginning to choke him.

"Is that the camera? I'm going to smash that over your fuckin' head."

"I haven't done anything."

"What's going on, Alan?" Another voice asked and Alan released his grip on Graham, who started coughing.

"This pervert's been taking pictures of the girls in the water."

"You're joking?"

"Look, there's the camera."

"Dirty bastard! Get him out the car."

Alan leant back in and grabbed Graham with even greater force.

"No! Stop! I haven't done anything! I can explain."

Graham landed roughly on the ground, Alan releasing his hold on him as he did so and diving back into the car to retrieve the camera. Graham slowly got to his knees and was immediately knocked back to the ground by a kick from Alan's accomplice, which connected with his jaw. More blows landed on his body as he tried to curl himself into a ball, each one accompanied by an angry shout.

"Pervert!"

"Bastard!"

"Beast!"

He heard the crunch just as the shoe connected with his head and he wasn't sure whether it was his skull or his camera which had broken. He wondered whether anyone witnessing the attack would think to get a camera out to capture the moment. It would make for a unique picture, he thought as he passed out.

Electric Barbarella

I wrote a two-chord song which I played to my family. Everyone applauded politely but I knew there was something missing.

"It's a bit too political," my dad said.

"It's a bit too naughty," my mum said.

"Can you play Electric Barbarella?" my gran asked.

"Sorry," I said. "I don't know that one. Who sings it?"

"Duran Duran. It's not one of their best-known songs, but it's still a great wee tune. You should learn it."

She started humming it.

"Maybe I will," I said.

I didn't have a title for my own song but the chorus went like this:

'Is that a weapon of mass destruction in your pocket or are you just pleased to see me?

If Hans Blix turned up on your doorstep would you invite him in for tea?

And if he discovered you'd run out of biscuits there would be a ruction.

So let me get my hands on your weapon of mass destruction.'

The chord change was from 'G' to 'C' every eight bars and when I played it in my bedroom it sounded fine.

"What about putting an A-minor in the middle?" my gran suggested. I just laughed but when I tried it, the difference was amazing.

95

"How did you know to do that?" I asked.

"Nick Rhodes told me," she said, winking at me.

"Who's he?"

She just smiled, and started humming the song again, and I guessed it was probably an old boyfriend she didn't want to talk about.

Save A Prayer

Michael Gallagher wrote a book and his wife left him. That was the edited version. Heather would be happy to provide the full, unabridged story to anyone who cared to listen. Blaming the book always seemed to be the easy option, though he knew it hadn't helped matters.

"I wish you hadn't written it, Michael." That's what she always said, a mantra that began every time she caught sight of a pile of the books stacked precariously in a corner of the living room.

"I had to," was his only line of defence.

A copy was lying on the kitchen table in front of him. He stared at the cover until he was convinced he could hear the seagulls that hovered in the background of the picture calling out to each other. He breathed in and smelt the salty air drifting off waves that seemed to lose energy and enthusiasm as they reached the shore.

It was his favourite photograph that he'd chosen for the cover. Sarah's face stared up at him. Smiling. She was kneeling beside a crooked sand-castle, plastic spade in hand, momentarily distracted from her construction work. She wore a Winnie the Pooh t-shirt that stretched to her knees. Her face was screwed up as she stared into the sun hovering in the sky behind Heather. It was taken on a day out at the seaside when she was about two-and-a-half-years-old. He was just behind her left shoulder, his forehead burning from the sun's rays. Later, he'd feel sick and dizzy and Heather would tell him off for not wearing a hat. The cover of the book was black and white except for Sarah.

It wasn't like writing the book was the first thing he did as soon as they came home from the funeral and closed the door on all the mourners who had crowded into their house over the previous few days. Suddenly it was just the two of them in a building which still echoed with the sound of Sarah's laughter and tears; he'd walk into a room expecting to hear her voice or perhaps stumble over toys that she'd discarded on the floor. Silences became longer and more awkward, bitter even, and something which he'd imagined had been built on the strongest of foundations was crumbling before his eyes.

They'd said 'for better, for worse,' but neither of them had ever imagined what that 'worse' would be. 'Until death do us part,' they'd repeated, staring into each other's eyes with a romantic naivety, not for a moment imagining that those words would come back to haunt them.

Putting pen to paper had been easier to do than he'd imagined. Words that could barely form in his mouth suddenly found substance on the page. It felt as if, every time the pen caressed the blank page of the notepad, an enormous weight was beginning to slowly lift from his shoulders. Before long, he had finished the story and transferred it to his laptop, reliving every painful word as he typed it up. The weight never fully left him. It was still with him now, but it definitely felt lighter, and almost bearable.

He didn't tell Heather what he was doing. It was only after the books were delivered that she found out. She knew he'd been writing about Sarah – she thought he was writing to their daughter – but she didn't know what it was until she saw the finished result. She'd walked into the living-room and nearly fell over the box of books. She peered inside and Sarah stared up at her, rows and rows of her. He hoped she was going to take a copy out and look at it. He'd held his breath for so long that he felt like he was gasping for air when he breathed out.

She looked at him but didn't say anything. It was like a stand-off from a cowboy film, two gunslingers just a few yards apart, eyes narrowed, hands poised at holsters, the wind stirring up the dust which swirled around well-worn leather boots, everybody peering out nervously from behind lace curtains or through the cracks of hastily closed doors. All it needed was the theme tune from *The Good, The Bad and The Ugly*. He blinked first. When he glanced up again, it was her back he saw, disappearing out the room and up the stairs. The inevitable questions followed later.

"Why did you write it, Michael?"

"I don't know. I had to."

"You had to? What does that mean? I don't understand. I didn't have to."

"I didn't want her to be forgotten."

She'd sprung up out of her chair like an athlete who'd just heard the starting pistol, and paced up and down the room.

"How could she be forgotten? How? I won't forget her. You won't forget her."

He'd shrugged. In his head the explanation was there and it made sense, but he knew it wouldn't sound the same if he said it out loud. He wanted there to be a permanent record of Sarah, not just in his mind, or Heather's, and not just stored in an old cardboard box full of photographs that he sometimes got out and cried over. He wanted people who knew her and those who didn't to find out what her life had been like, short and painful and bleak as it often was.

He had to tell her story. Her first tooth. Her first word. The day she tottered between chair and couch unaided. Her shrieks of joy as he pushed her back and forth on a swing in a park near their house. Walking hand in hand along the street to buy sweets at the local newsagent's shop, a constant stream of words floating in the air, a thousand questions which he never tired of answering. How does an aeroplane fly? Why do dogs bark? Is there really a wee green man in the traffic lights? Is it true that if you eat the skin off apples you die?

He wanted to tell about all the bad stuff too. Blood tests and x-rays. Operations. Sitting at her bedside and praying to a God he didn't believe existed that she would survive. Hopes of a transplant. The despair of another letdown. Trying to explain what was happening in words that a four-year-old might understand. Sitting in the house alone or attempting to dredge up a conversation with Heather at the side of Sarah's hospital bed when neither of them could bear the sound of the other's voice.

And he wanted to explain that when she died, her eyes closed and her face relaxed, her lips curling up into a smile like she was dreaming about that trip to the seaside and of eating an ice-cream cone. Maybe it was just relief that the pain had finally gone? It felt as if someone had thrust a fist into his chest and ripped out his heart. Her first word was 'Dada.'

"I wish you hadn't written it, Michael."

"Sorry."

"She was my daughter too."

He picked up the book from the table and put it into the rucksack along with the other five copies he'd already placed there. Even the title had annoyed Heather. *Daddy's Girl.* It was as if he was trying to monopolise Sarah's life and the parental grief that came with her death. That's what Heather told him, and even when he tried to disagree, he knew it wouldn't change how she felt about it. That's what people used to call Sarah. 'She's a real daddy's girl,' they would say whenever she took his hand or sat on his knee or cried and held out her arms for him to pick her up. He always liked it whenever someone said that.

He hadn't realised he'd wanted to be a father until Heather was pregnant. It was actually the first time he felt the bump – Sarah – moving. Then he knew it was all he ever wanted to be. When Sarah was born, the midwife gently placed her in his arms, offering a reassuring smile as he stared at the tiny screaming creature with a mixture of awe and terror. 'Talk to her,' she said and he did. Quietly, almost embarrassed, he said her name. 'Sarah.' Then she stopped crying. As if by magic. There was silence like she'd recognised her daddy's voice and she knew she was safe. He realised then that he could never love anyone the way he loved his daughter.

The words he'd read in the various books he and Heather had poured over, as if any book could really prepare them for becoming parents, seemed to be true. He had talked to his unborn child, sang to her, told her he loved her and that she was 'Daddy's baby,' because the baby would recognise his voice once it was born. And she did.

He'd wanted to shout to Heather and tell her but he sensed, as she mustered up an exhausted smile while nurses continued to hover round her, that she would be neither interested nor impressed. So he kept talking to his daughter, and she remained quiet and content.

Sarah. Her name seemed to fit perfectly, like the white baby-grow outfit the midwife had dressed her in. If anyone had asked him at that precise moment what other names had been in the frame, he couldn't have told them. It no longer mattered. There was only one name. Sarah.

Michael's weekends now followed the same pattern, like it was a ritual he felt compelled to undertake the way other people went shopping or to the football, or spent the day nursing hangovers from the night before. No-one had wanted to publish his book so he'd printed it himself, but the bookshops hadn't been interested in stocking it when he asked them. So every Saturday, he visited bookshops and left copies on the shelves. The shops didn't know he did this, though he was sure they'd be happy enough to take the money if somebody decided to buy a copy. He didn't care about the money. He just wanted people to read about Sarah.

The rest of the week was just a hindrance, minutes and hours and days which stood between him and what he really wanted to do. Even when he was at work, his mind would wander. One minute he'd be talking about Shakespeare, aware of the blank, spotty faces staring up at him or gazing out the window, the next he was picturing himself standing in the middle of a bookshop, surrounded on all sides by shelves that stretched from floor to ceiling. He'd be holding a copy of his book, looking for the appropriate place to slide it in. What if all those books suddenly toppled off the shelves? A sudden tremor might dislodge them, or someone colliding with the shelf from behind, and he'd be buried beneath millions of words. Perhaps no-one would realise he was there until the staff eventually began clearing up.

Then he was back in the classroom, standing silently beside his desk, a copy of *A Midsummer Night's Dream* lying open in the palm of his hand. He'd stare at the page for a few moments, trying to re-focus on the words and wracking his brain to remember what was the last thing he'd said. Everyone would stare at him, not wanting to break the silence. They were curious to see how long this trance would last. He never knew whether it was seconds or minutes, though he was aware of it happening more and more.

In truth, while he still looked forward to the weekend, there was no longer the same thrill to his task. He hadn't been able to replicate the feeling of exhilaration which was his companion as he trekked from shop to shop that first day.

The Waterstones store in Sauchiehall Street was his first port of call. It was always crowded, providing a welcoming degree of anonymity. The heavy rain was also pushing some passers-by into the store for shelter, and he had to jostle his way through a few people who had congregated near the front door. It was a typical Glasgow day, the grey sky spewing out a constant stream of rain on to the streets and buildings and cars and people. The hiss of traffic was absent from this pedestrianised section of the city centre, but there was still the occasional rumble of raindrops clattering off the tops of umbrellas clutched by those who declined the refuge offered by the array of stores lining either side of the street, instead determined to carry on, regardless. They were true Glaswegians. The city would grind to a halt if everyone refused to venture out any time it rained.

A few assistants gathered at the cash till on each floor, visibly annoyed whenever their conversations were interrupted by a customer. One girl sat behind a computer at the end of a long counter on the ground floor under a sign hanging from the ceiling which read 'Customer Services'. Michael watched her for a few minutes, punching the keyboard aggressively and then peering at the screen before pointing in the general direction of where he presumed the book in question might be found.

He wandered round the ground floor of the store, picking up a book every now and then and glancing quickly at the words on the back page before putting it down. There were tables full of offers.

'BUY ONE, GET ONE FREE.'

'50% OFF.'

'THREE FOR THE PRICE OF TWO.'

People always flocked round those tables. One time he bought three books on offer, barely bothering to check what they were. He was never going to read them anyway. It was the stickers he was after. When he got home, he carefully peeled off the first one and then stuck it on his own book, smoothing down the edges so it didn't come loose or fall off. He did the same with the other two, and then put an Oxford Dictionary and a book about the Spanish Inquisition on top of them. The heavy tomes pressed down on his flimsy publication overnight and he was pleased with the results when he checked the following morning. He could hardly wait to get into town that day. He was confident someone would buy one of those books. Everyone loved a bargain.

He made his way up to the second floor where all the academic books were housed. It was quieter and he strolled along each aisle, unzipping his rucksack as he arrived back at the stairs. By the time he walked down to the next floor, he was clutching two copies of his own book. Anyone looking at him would presume he'd picked them up somewhere else in the shop. He started at the beginning of the fiction books – 'A' for Achebe – and slowly made his way along the shelves, feigning interest in what they held as he glided towards 'G'. He'd always figured that more people browsed through this area of the store, even though his own book would be classed as non-fiction.

Once there, he took advantage of the fact no-one else was in the aisle and quickly made a space on the shelf. He pushed his books in at the correct alphabetical position, and then checked to see whether any had been bought since his last visit. There were three copies of *Daddy's Girl*. He slid the two new ones in alongside their siblings and walked away with a smile. Another one had found a home. Somewhere in Glasgow it was lying at the side of a bed, a bookmark slid between the pages; he couldn't bear the thought of the person being a page folder.

After putting the copies on the shelf, he moved away and stopped in the front of a section housing Mills & Boon romances. As he zipped up the rucksack and slung it over his shoulder, he glanced over and saw someone pick out a copy of *Daddy's Girl*. His heart missed a beat. He'd read that phrase a million times before but never realised until this moment how that felt, like slowly reaching the top of a rollercoaster and soaking in an incredible view stretching out for miles before looking down at the sheer drop. There was a moment of panic, terror, excitement and anticipation all rolled into one before the machine plummeted at speed towards what you prayed were more twists and turns and not a painful and crushing demise.

It was a girl who studied the book. She was young. In her twenties, he guessed. She wore a sky blue t-shirt with 'LOVE' emblazoned across the front in sparkling, fake jewels. It was short enough to expose her tanned midriff, which was probably fake as well. Her bare feet peeked out from under her jeans. She was wearing sandals, but he noticed a small shamrock tattoo on the front of each foot. A pair of sunglasses were propped optimistically on top of her bleached blonde head, though wayward strands of brown hair betrayed its original colour. She'd finished reading the back cover and was flicking through the pages. He tried to guess what part she was at. He edged a little nearer. The girl had closed the book but held on to it, shuffling along the aisle but throwing only cursory glances at everything else on offer. He was in the aisle as well now, and looked up at the shelf just to make sure his eyes hadn't deceived him. The girl had reached the end and started back towards him.

"What book have you got there?" he blurted out as she reached him.

The girl stopped. She looked flustered, not sure if she'd done something wrong. Traces of panic began spreading across her face. She glanced at the book and held it up but said nothing.

"What made you choose that one?" He was surprised at his own boldness, but it was an opportunity he couldn't pass up.

"I thought it looked good," she mumbled.

"Good?"

"Sad."

She looked at the book again and then up at him, repeating the action several times, a frown appearing on her face like a baby seeing its reflection in the mirror.

"Is this your book?" she asked in an anxious whisper the way his mum uttered the word 'homosexual'.

He nodded.

"Wow."

The girl seemed stunned to have met a real live author, as if she couldn't grasp the sudden realisation that books didn't just appear on the shelves by magic.

"I'm glad you decided to buy it," he said.

"It looks good."

"I hope you like it."

"I'm sure I will... Oh!" she gasped. "That's your daughter."

He nodded.

"That's so sad," she said, her face suddenly adopting an expression of sympathy he despised whenever it was thrown at him. He realised people didn't know what to say. Family, friends, work colleagues. Even he and Heather hadn't been able to find the right words, or any words, to say to each other. The truth was, there was nothing to say. Ever. Nothing anyone could say would ever make a difference and he could never offer anything in return. Just silence. Heather had suggested they speak to someone, in the dim and distant past when she was still trying to save what remained of their marriage. He'd dismissed the idea immediately.

He looked at the girl again, still holding his book nervously. "I hope you enjoy it," he muttered, beginning to walk away.

"Wait," she said, almost too loud. "Will you sign it for me?"

"You want me to sign it?"

"If you don't mind? I'll just go over and pay for it first."

She nodded towards the three members of staff at the cash till, two girls comparing lip piercings, while a guy, all spots and out of control curly hair, said something which made them laugh.

"Do you want to come over with me?" the girl said.

"I'll just sign it now. I'm sure the shop won't mind. You're buying it anyway," he said, reluctant to attract any unwanted attention.

"Okay," she shrugged. He held *Daddy's Girl* in his hand, staring at the front cover. It was his book, yet this copy no longer felt like his. It was somebody else's now, or soon would be once the girl paid for it.

He studied the cover again, staring at his daughter's smiling face. It was a trip to Troon on a sunny June day. The sunshine, as welcome as it was unexpected, saw them eager not to pass up the opportunity and they headed half-an-hour down the coast. The beach seemed to stretch for miles in either direction and while there were other families who'd all arrived with the same aim in mind, vast tracts of the sand remained unoccupied. They had build sand-castles, paddled in the water's edge – it was sunny but the Irish Sea remained cold and uninviting – and later bought ice-cream cones which they ate while sitting on the wall above the beach, staring out at the water and the shadow of Paddy's Milestone in the distance, Sarah safely sandwiched in between her mum and dad. Heather had taken the picture. She always preferred to be behind the camera rather than in front of it, while Sarah was able to conjure up the perfect smile the instant she saw the lens pointed at her.

"Do you have a pen?" he asked the girl.

"I think so. I'm sure there's one in here," she said, rummaging in her bag. She handed him a blue pen. He opened up the cover and moved the pen towards the inside page.

"What's your name?"

"Courtney."

"How do you spell that?"

"C-O-U-R-T-N-E-Y."

He paused and then wrote, *'To Courtney. Thanks for buying my book. I wish I never had to write it but I hope you enjoy it anyway. Best wishes. Michael Gallagher.'*

If he was signing hundreds, he would have kept the message brief, but this was his first one and he wanted it to be meaningful. She took the book back with a grateful smile, immediately reading the inscription.

"Thanks," she said.

There was nothing else to say. He left her and

walked back to the ground floor and then out into the street, not caring that the rain remained as persistent as before. He didn't feel quite as elated as he imagined he would have been in meeting someone who was buying his book. There were two more bookshops to visit and he wanted to do this as quickly as possible. Once the rucksack was empty there would be nothing left to distract him. It would be time to meet Heather.

It was a small office and Michael felt like he was back at school, sitting nervously in the headmaster's room, waiting for his arrival and worrying about the range of possible punishments that might be meted out to him. He knew he wasn't going to get punished now – he hadn't really done anything wrong, for a start – but there was still a residual feeling of guilt in his mind. Or was it simply annoyance at having been caught? After all this time, he'd thought of himself as an expert, slipping in and out of shops unnoticed. Maybe confidence had bred complacency?

It had been the last place he visited. Chapter and Verse. It was a small shop, buried away on the edge of town, probably to try and avoid the exorbitant rent and rates that city centre businesses were charged. Everything was on the ground floor except for a small, first-floor area which housed the children's section. Michael had never gone up the wooden stairs. The lure of bright colours and fancy posters adorning the walls, or the noise of excited children reading and chatting and laughing and crying, which floated down to the ground floor, was all too easy to resist.

The till-point was in the middle of the ground floor, surrounded on all sides by shelves packed with books. There was not enough space to house all the stock, so piles of books littered the floor. Sometimes it felt like an obstacle course, clambering over books and side-stepping readers as he ventured further into the shop. There was always music playing, which floated along the low ceiling and filled up the entire area of the shop. He recognised the theme tune from *The Godfather*. He'd always imagined that it would be distracting. He never liked any noise when he was reading, but it felt strangely relaxing and unobtrusive. There was a sense that this was a real book shop, for real readers.

He'd visited before on a number of occasions, and not always to leave his own book. Sometimes he just passed the time, maybe as long as an hour, browsing the shelves. Occasionally he would even buy a book, or several if they caught his eye, but while he might head home with the best of intentions to start reading, his new purchases merely joined the stack of books already gathered at the side of the bed which he'd bought before with a similar determination.

He only had one copy of his book left in the rucksack, and he knew exactly where to leave it. He didn't want to just charge in and head straight for the appropriate place, so instead he shuffled round the shop, picking out books at random, sometimes just examining the cover, other times reading the words on the back, though each time he returned it to the shelf. The music continued in the background. Paul McCartney singing *Live And Let Die*. It wasn't his favourite James Bond theme tune, though. That had to be *A View To A Kill*.

There was one member of staff at the till, sitting on what Michael presumed had previously been a bar stool and reading *The Great Gatsby*. He was bald and wore glasses with a thick black frame. Occasionally he'd stroke his thin goatee beard as he turned a page, like he was contemplating what he'd just read. Michael smiled. This was how he imagined book shop staff should look like, right down to the black t-shirt with an Oscar Wilde quote on the back – 'We are all in the gutter, but some of us are looking at the stars.'

As he moved past the till, the man looked up and nodded before returning to his book. There had been a time when the prospect of working in a bookshop would have appealed to Michael. There were still days now, when he was trying to extol the merits of First World War poetry to a class of thirteen-year-olds, when it seemed like a better career choice. Of course, he knew it wasn't all about sitting reading your favourite book while strangers perused the shelves, but at least when his back was turned, the shop assistant didn't have a teenage voice, hovering on the precipice of puberty, shout out 'Wanker!' to the amusement of his classmates.

At first, when that had happened to him, Michael would demand to know the identity of the culprit, only to be met by the proverbial wall of silence. Then, he began to single out who he thought it might be, which still didn't elicit any admission of guilt. Eventually, he realised the solution was to punish the girls. He would pick one at random and make her stand out in the corridor for the duration of the lesson. The result was generally angry fingers pointed in the direction of the guilty party by the girl and her outraged friends.

Michael had drifted towards the back of the shop, the copy of *Daddy's Girl* now in his hand, while the empty rucksack hung listlessly over his shoulder. He reached 'G' in the fiction section and noticed there was one copy of his book on the shelf. That meant two had been bought since his last visit. Smiling, he slipped the copy he was holding on to the shelf.

"What are you doing?" a voice said and he turned round. It was the bald shop assistant. The accent surprised him. He'd imagined a soft, gentle tone, perhaps from the south of England, but this was harsh and confrontational. Pure Glaswegian.

"Just putting the book back," Michael said.

The assistant stretched across him and removed both copies of *Daddy's Girl*. He glanced at the cover and then at Michael. "You better come through to the manager's office," he said.

Michael was still in the office. Waiting. He didn't know why he had meekly agreed to the assistant's request. He could just as easily have refused and stormed out of the shop in a fit of false pique. He hadn't done anything wrong, in that he hadn't stolen anything, so he had nothing to answer for, but he'd simply acquiesced. Perhaps it was the voice, which carried a hint of menace that Michael still felt was out of place in these surroundings. It had sounded less like a request and more of an order, and so he had meekly followed the man towards the door at the back of the shop, the one marked 'PRIVATE', and stepped through into a warren of offices, store rooms, kitchen and toilet.

Five minutes passed, then another five, before he remembered about Heather. He was late for his meeting with her, and she always hated it when anyone was late, particularly him. He took out his mobile phone and quickly typed a message and sent it to her. There was no point trying to explain what had happened. It would take too long and if he mentioned the book, it would only make her angrier instead of more understanding.

It was Heather who had wanted to see him. She'd suggested it at the cemetery when they'd seen each other. It had been an accidental encounter. Most times when he visited Sarah, he was on his own. Only on special occasions – her birthday, Christmas Day, her anniversary – did they go together. When he saw Heather already at the graveside, kneeling down and re-arranging the flowers in the plastic vases surrounding the white marble headstone, taking out the ones which had withered and replacing them with fresh ones she'd brought with her, he was tempted to turn and leave. She hadn't seen him yet and he thought it might be easier to return later.

He'd glanced to his left. An old man stood in front of a mound of freshly stacked earth. He leant on a walking stick and stared at the ground like he was waiting for something to happen; a resurrection perhaps or maybe he was hoping he would be swallowed up in order that his pain would be eased. His back was curved like he was burdened with an invisible weight on his shoulders, and wisps of grey hair were occasionally disturbed by the gentle breeze which glided silently through the cemetery.

Michael turned back towards Heather, who was looking at him. She offered a weak smile and he knew he couldn't walk away now. He'd asked her why she wanted to meet him, but she said it wasn't the time or the place. He briefly contemplated refusing to meet unless she explained, but he knew it wasn't the time or the place for that kind of behaviour either. Instead, they stood side by side, careful to avoid any contact, and stared at the headstone, studying the black lettering, sometimes with an intensity that suggested they were burning the words permanently into their minds, or else wearing bemused expressions, like they'd set eyes on indecipherable hieroglyphics. The symbols never changed.

SARAH ELIZABETH GALLAGHER

The other words recorded the details — mere details — of a life that was over in the blink of an eye. No-one ventured close enough to discover who they mourned for, though if they did, they would surely back away as soon as they knew. For what was there to say to the grieving parents of a four-year-old girl?

The office door opened and Michael looked round. A woman walked in, closed the door behind her and sat down at the other side of the desk. She was dressed all in black except for a large white badge that read 'World's Best Mummy' in bold green letters. It looked as though a child had written it but that might have been a deliberate design gimmick.

"I'm Grace Donnelly, I'm the manager here." She held out her hand which he shook gently. Her nail polish was also black. "So this is your book?"

She took one of the copies that was on her desk and held it up. He shrugged.

"This has been an absolute mystery to us," she said with a laugh. "We've sold two copies – both on the same day, actually – and we had no idea where they came from. No record of ordering them. No mention of who the publisher is. At least you put a price on the cover, which was something... This is your book, I take it?"

"Yes."

"And you just left it on our shelves?"

He nodded.

"Why?"

"Because I wanted people to read it."

Grace sat back, still holding the book, and looked at the cover. Michael studied her. He wondered what age she was. His guess was early thirties, though he'd never been much good with ages, so she could be anything from twenty-one to forty. She wore the lightest touch of make-up, as if the brush had barely caressed her skin, though there was still enough to give her cheeks a healthy glow. She'd saved all her efforts for applying lipstick, which was bright red. Her lips were mesmerising. Her hair was black and was tied lazily in a pony-tail.

"The thing is..." she looked at the cover again, "... Michael Gallagher, you can't just come in to the shop and put your books on our shelves. We need to know what we're selling, and have a record of all our stock. If you wanted us to take your book, you should have sent it in to us and if we liked it then we might have bought some copies."

"But I did."

"What?"

"I sent it to you."

"Did you really? I'm sure I would have

remembered. We get everything delivered here and either I go through them or Joe does," she said, nodding towards the door. Michael presumed she was talking about the goatee-bearded assistant who'd caught him.

"Well, I definitely sent a copy to you but I never heard anything back from anyone. So I thought this would be the next best thing."

"But what about the money?"

"I paid for them all myself."

"No, I mean, the money from us selling the book. Normally the publisher gets some of that."

"I don't care about the money. I just want people to read the book."

Grace began reading the back cover, her eyes quickly scanning the words that he'd laboured over in the hope that they summed up what the book was about. If she asked, he was sure he'd be able to recite the entire text.

'Sarah Elizabeth Gallagher was a beautiful little girl whose parents loved her very much. From the moment she was born, she brought great love and joy into the lives of everyone who knew her. Sadly, Sarah's life was short, and often painful. After a brave and courageous battle with cancer, Sarah sadly passed away at the age of four.

The pain of her loss is something that could never be explained in the pages of any book, but Daddy's Girl records and recounts those four years in loving detail – the laughter and the tears.

Sarah Elizabeth Gallagher had a smile which could light up a room and her courage throughout her illness was an inspiration to everyone who was lucky enough to know her. This is Sarah's story ... the story of an all-too-short life, but one that will never be forgotten.'

Grace sighed as she put the book back on top of the other copy. She smiled and Michael found himself staring at her lips, watching them as they moved.

"I don't know what to say," the lips said.

"That's okay. There's nothing to say."

"My daughter's six. Eva. She's in primary one." Grace held out a framed photograph that was sitting on the desk.

He glanced at the picture. He suddenly felt a tightening across his chest as if he was being bound by a heavy rope and he was struggling to breath. Was this how a heart attack felt like? The little girl in the picture sat on a carousel horse. She was waving at the camera while her other hand clutched the pole that stretched to the roof of the fairground ride. Her smile seemed nervous, as if she couldn't wait to grab the pole with both hands again.

"That's a nice name." He didn't know what else to say. He didn't like talking about other people's children because he was scared the emotions he had spent days and weeks and months trying to smother would resurface. It was nearly two-and-a-half-years – eight hundred and thirty-one days to be precise – since Sarah died, and it turned out that time was not a great healer.

"That's my favourite picture," Grace said.

"It's lovely."

"If I had to choose a picture for the cover of a book about Eva, it would be that one."

"I hope you never have to."

"Me too. I can't imagine what that must feel like. I think it's amazing you get through a single day. I'd just give up."

"You'd be surprised."

There had been times when he had thought of giving up. Once or twice. He never told Heather about it. It was difficult enough for her trying to cope with the loss of her daughter without having to deal with him as well. For all he knew, she might have felt the same way. Sometimes, though, just when he thought he was managing to get through the days and weeks, he'd be dragged down again; the sight of a child walking hand-in-hand with their father; cuddly toys in the window of a shop he was walking past; the chimes of an ice-cream van a few streets away. Then he'd be stopped in his tracks, literally, like someone had pressed a 'pause' button. There would be the doubt; did it really happen? The disbelief; how had he managed to keep going? The despair; how could he go on?

Grace picked up the book again and studied the front cover. "She's a beautiful little girl."

He resisted the temptation to correct her. She *was* a beautiful little girl.

"It is so sad," she said, sighing again. That was all anyone could really say. There were no words of solace, even though some people tried desperately to search for them. What inevitably came out were the clichés of grief, and they offered no comfort at all.

Grace picked up the books and held them out to Michael.

"Do you want me to take them back?"

"Yes," she laughed.

"You don't want to keep them and sell them?"

"Sorry."

He shrugged as he reluctantly took the books off her. He put them back on the desk, where they perched on the edge, as he picked up his rucksack and then dropped them into it. "I only wanted people to read about her," he said, almost in a whisper and Grace nodded with a smile. She stood up, which was his invitation to do the same.

"It was nice to meet you, Michael," she said, holding out her hand, which he shook.

"You too."

As she moved round the desk towards the door, he took a book from the rucksack and held it out to her.

"I told you, we can't stock it," she said with a laugh that betrayed the merest hint of impatience.

"It's for you," he said. "Just read it."

She hesitated, her eyes fixed on the cover.

"Please."

"Okay," she said, taking the copy and putting it on the desk beside the picture of her daughter. It was one less copy and one more reader.

The Wild Boys

A re we leaving, Danny?"

"Yes, Kevin, we're leaving."

"I like it here."

"I know."

"Can we stay? I'll be good, Danny. Promise."

"You are good, Kevin, but we still have to go."

Kevin stood at the window picking his nose and examining his finger. I sighed and kept packing. Last week I would have told him off, maybe even slapped his hand away. Not too hard, mind you, I didn't want him to start crying. It just didn't help if people saw him.

I could smell their pity hanging in the air like a really bad fart and I wanted to tell them they were wrong about Kevin. He was smart and funny and clever – well, maybe not that clever – but he wasn't stupid. Just because he wobbled when he walked and his arm seemed to dangle like a broken branch and he talked like he was drunk even though he was only eight, it didn't mean he was stupid.

"Beckham! Beckham!"

Kevin started banging on the glass and laughing.

"Beckham's home. Look, Danny. Come here. Look."

"I'm busy, Kevin."

"Look, Danny," he squealed, thumping the window again.

I could hear the dog barking but Kevin still wanted me to see for myself. The Alsatian was at the bottom of the garden, its front paws propped up on the wooden fence and it was barking at something next door. I knew it meant Sean was back.

Sean lived here. This was his home, his family, and he didn't like us invading it. He told me that the first night we arrived. I was on the top bunk and Kevin was already snoring below me when Sean hissed across the room.

"I hate you."

"What?"

"I hate you."

"You ate me?"

"Hate! I hate you."

"You ate poo?"

"You! I hate you."

I could see his agitated body in the darkness. He sat up and edged closer to the end of the bed. The wall behind him thudded and a muffled voice told us to get to sleep and I lay back with a smile.

Sean was twelve, a year older than me, but I was almost as tall as him so he didn't scare me. There had been a few fights in the three weeks we'd been here. Nothing serious, just pushing mainly, with a couple of half-hearted punches thrown for show. I would have beaten him in a real fight but it was probably better it had never gone that far.

It was usually Kevin who was the cause of our disagreements. Sean didn't like him. The first night we had dinner I watched as he became more horrified with each mouthful of mince and tatties that Kevin shovelled into his mouth. Admittedly, it wasn't the prettiest sight, like watching my gran eating a banana without her teeth in. A mouth with a mind of its own.

Mrs Donnelly had made the food especially for us.

Jacqui had told her it was our favourite. I remembered my mum making it, the way she'd help us mix it all together – mince, tatties and beans – to make a big brown mountain. I always licked my plate clean which made her laugh. I even remembered my dad putting some on a slice of bread to eat once he'd demolished the rest.

"That's disgusting, Gerry," my mum would say to him.

"I know, but it tastes good," he'd mumble through a mouthful of food.

She always said that's where I got it from – the mince and tatties sandwich – on the rare occasions she mentioned him at all. Maybe that's what I remembered? Not him eating but my mum talking about it later.

Mr and Mrs Donnelly had stared as I spread out the food on the bread, Mrs Donnelly with a look that would make you think I was smearing shite on it. I didn't care. My dad was right. It did taste good.

Sean didn't want us here, but maybe I'd have been the same if two strangers suddenly came to live in my house and sleep in my room and play with my toys and share my mum and dad?

He hated the fact we were in his room. It was massive, far too big for just one person but he obviously preferred it that way. A set of bunk beds had been erected against the wall opposite his bed and that's where Kevin and I slept. There was an invisible barrier drawn across the room that was meant to keep us away from him. He didn't let us on the PlayStation. He grabbed toys out of our hands, hid things away in the wardrobe if he saw either of us eyeing them up, but still we seemed to annoy him. I tried to make sure we stayed out of his way but it was difficult, especially at night.

Sean stood at the bedroom door, wearing a triumphant grin. He knew we were leaving today.

"I want to see Beckham," Kevin said and rushed towards the door.

"Be careful going down the stairs," I warned.

Sean didn't move and Kevin tried to squeeze past him without success.

"Let him out," I said, zipping up the bag and walking round the bed.

"What do you say, Kevin?" he said, folding his arms.

"Scuse me, Sean."

"Pardon?"

"Scuse me, Sean."

"What did you say?"

"SEAN!" I shouted.

"Scuse me, Sean."

"Oh sorry, Kevin. I didn't understand you there. I only speak English."

He stepped aside and Kevin disappeared out the room. I heard the thud of his feet as he raced downstairs and I waited for him crashing to the bottom, but the fall never came. Only barking and Kevin shouting "Beckham! Beckham!"

Kevin loved dogs and dogs loved him. They never made fun of his speech or the way he walked. He was nice to them and that was enough. We never had a dog. My mum hated them. She said they made the house smell like a toilet. But Mrs Gallagher downstairs had a Highland terrier, a white one that barked from the moment it woke up in the morning until it went to sleep at night. She would let it out in the back garden when we were playing and Kevin would forget whatever it was we were doing and start pestering it. Scotty, it was called.

Mum used to warn us to stay away from it.

"They're vicious wee things," she'd say. "They'll bite you as soon as look at you."

Scotty would growl at me sometimes but never at Kevin. They were the best of pals.

"That wasn't funny, Sean," I said turning to him.

"I think it was."

"You're just an idiot."

"And you're so gay, Danny."

I grabbed the bag off the bed and strode to the door, determined for one last fight if Sean tried to block me. This time I would punch him in the face. Hard. He leant against the frame, still smiling.

"Bye, Danny."

I stuck my middle finger up and walked past him. I was halfway down the stairs when he shouted, "And say goodbye to Thevthen."

I stopped. I was tempted to go back but Jacqui would hear about it later and that would make it harder to find another family to take us because they'd discover that I was a troublemaker, and I'd feel guilty because Kevin and I would be stuck in the home forever. I walked downstairs and into the kitchen where Mrs Donnelly sat with a cup of tea.

She looked like a mum. There were no trendy clothes or fancy hair-do, or make-up plastered on her face. She didn't smoke and I never saw her drink, and she would give Sean a cuddle when he came in from school or a kiss on his forehead when he was lying in bed. He hated that. The fact we saw he was a mummy's boy. I never said anything, just sneered, but it must have been nice to have someone like that.

Kevin would sometimes ask me to tell him about our mum. He forgot things, how she looked or what she sounded like so I had to keep reminding him. I had a couple of pictures that he would hold while I was talking. In one she was sitting on a couch in our old house. She had a bottle of beer in one hand, a cigarette in the other, and she was laughing, as if whoever was taking the picture had said something really funny. Her mouth was wide open and you could see her black teeth.

The second picture was taken on a beach. It must have been a cold and windy day because she had a coat on and her black hair was all over the place but she was smiling and she looked pretty and happy and young. She was crouched down beside a buggy and a tiny face peered out from a mass of clothes and covers. It was me. She had written on the back of the picture, *Ayr, July 15th, 2004*. I was one-year-old. Kevin wasn't even born. My dad had taken the picture. Kevin always asked where he was and I told him he'd gone swimming with the dolphins while we all watched from the beach.

I loved to see his eyes widen and a crooked grin crack across his face as if he actually remembered it himself. The pictures helped me. I could make up different stories every time Kevin asked. He was none the wiser. It didn't really matter what I told him. It was better than the truth. Kevin was lucky he didn't remember that.

Mrs Donnelly sipped her tea, peering over the edge of the mug with guilty eyes. Mr Donnelly had said goodbye before he went to work. He shook my hand and ruffled Kevin's hair and told us we were good boys. Kevin smiled and said "Fanks, Mr Donnelly," but I was silent. I'd heard it all before.

Mrs Donnelly smiled awkwardly as I sat down opposite her.

"Jacqui'll be here soon," she said. I nodded. I could see Kevin playing in the garden with Beckham. The dog was lying on its back and Kevin was tickling it, then it would spring to its feet and lick his face. It was disgusting but it made him laugh.

"I'm sorry it didn't work out, Danny. You're both lovely boys."

I shrugged.

"Sean will miss you. I think he's liked having you here. Like a couple of wee brothers."

I snorted and her eyes widened but I knew she wouldn't say the obvious, like 'What's the matter, Danny?' because she didn't care. Not really. Once the front door closed over behind us, she would breathe a sigh of relief that everything was back to 'normal'.

Sean probably said something to them or maybe they just realised it themselves, but she would have made the phone call to Jacqui when we were at school or in bed. It was as easy as that.

Kevin's laughter was getting louder. He was excited. People always stared when they heard him. It started off really deep, which sounded strange for someone his age, then it slowly got higher, as if it was being stretched like an elastic band, until he sounded like a girl. It usually made me laugh too but not today. The doorbell rang and I knew it was Jacqui.

While Mrs Donnelly answered the door, I walked outside to get Kevin. I stood with my hands in my pockets and watched him rolling about the grass with Beckham. I didn't know what I'd miss about this place, if anything. It was okay, as far as foster homes went. We'd been in better. More often than not, we'd been in worse. I could never understand why the people in those houses seemed to hate us. I thought they volunteered to look after us. At least Mr and Mrs Donnelly weren't like that.

Maybe they always wanted more children but they couldn't so they were trying us out for size? If Sean wasn't so annoying I would have felt sorry for him. I would have hated being an only child, all alone in that giant room with no-one else to play with. Even when dad left, and then mum had to go away, I had Kevin and he had me. That would never change.

"Kevin, it's time to go home," I said, struggling to make myself heard over the duet of Beckham's bark and my brother's laugh. Beckham would miss Kevin. At least someone in the house would.

"Kevin!"

Kevin looked round as Beckham ran a big pink slobbery tongue down his cheek.

"Beckham! Stop," he said, wrapping his arm round the dog's neck to control its head.

"We've got to go now, Kevin. Jacqui's here."

"Can we take Beckham?"

"Beckham stays here, Kevin. This is his home."

"I don't want to go."

He squeezed the dog tightly and Beckham struggled to break free. Kevin didn't realise his own strength. His face scrunched up and he looked away from me. I crouched down beside him and gently touched his shoulder. He flinched. This happened every time.

"Kevin, we're going home. Jacqui's going to drive us there."

"I want to stay here. With Beckham."

"But there's not enough room here."

"I'll sleep in the bunky bed. You go on top."

"But Sean needs his room for all his stuff."

Kevin's frown got deeper and he started breathing quickly through his nose. Beckham had managed to escape and backed off, perhaps sensing the change in mood or not relishing the prospect of another attempted strangulation.

"We can come back and visit Beckham," I said. What was one more lie? Kevin looked round, his face immediately relaxing.

"Can we take him walks? To the park?"

"Yes, we'll take him to the park."

Kevin's head bobbed back and forth like a little nodding toy in the back of a moving car.

"Come on, let's go." I tapped his arm and helped him to his feet, brushing bits of grass off his clothes.

"I like it here," he said as we walked to the back door, Beckham trotting along beside us.

"I know, I know. Maybe next time we'll find somewhere we don't have to leave."

"We can stay forever?"

"Forever."

"And Beckham can visit?"

I laughed. "Yes, Beckham can visit."

"Will they be nice?"

"Who?"

"The people who'll dopt us."

"I hope so, Kevin. I hope so."

I could see Jacqui through the window, talking to Mrs Donnelly and glancing out towards us every few seconds. She was always trying to find a family who'd take us both – I wouldn't go anywhere without Kevin – but I think she was secretly glad when she got the call to come and take us back. I would never tell her, but I was glad to see her too.

"Sean! Sean! Come on downstairs and say goodbye. Danny and Kevin are leaving."

We all stood at the front door and looked up the stairs, waiting for Sean to appear.

"I'll just go up and say goodbye, Mrs Donnelly," I said and took the stairs two at a time before anyone could object.

"What a nice boy," I heard her tell Jacqui.

I opened Sean's door and he looked up. He was sitting in front of the TV.

"What do you want?" he said.

"Just to say goodbye."

"Goodbye and good riddance to you and your spazzy brother. Now I've got my own room back."

"Hey, Sean."

"What?"

"I saw your mum's tits."

"What?"

"She let me see them. Said if I paid her a pound she'd show me them, so I did. I took the money out of your money bank."

He glared at me as his face turned a furious red.

"You stole my money? MUM!"

I raced back downstairs and grabbed the bag.

"He says bye," I mumbled, barging past Jacqui, who was holding the door open while Mrs Donnelly stared towards Sean's shrieking voice.

All the way home Jacqui fired questions at me but I ducked out the way of every one. Kevin just stared out the window, pressing his head against the cold glass and occasionally muttering "I miss Beckham."

Someone Else Not Me

When I sleep I dream of the swimming pool. I'm standing at the edge, staring at the clear blue water. The sun is burning my back. Laura tells me to put some cream on first. A man throws a ball to his teenage son who jumps up to catch it and then plunges under the water. A young couple tread water at the side. The girl, blonde hair tied back in a ponytail, has her arms wrapped round his neck and they're kissing. Two little girls, both wearing identical pink armbands, run up and down the side, laughing and squealing as their mum gently splashes them from the pool.

I push my feet closer to the edge until my toes caress the water. It feels cool. Soothing. I imagine my body breaking the surface as I glide underneath before emerging further up the pool. I crouch over, then change my mind and take a few steps back. Laura's still shouting at me. I turn round and see her waving a bottle of sun cream. I nod and mouth, 'In a minute.'

I sprint forward and leap off the edge, outstretched arms leading the way as I disappear. I always wake up when I hit the concrete bottom of the pool.

I lie in bed, sweat pouring down my face, t-shirt clinging to my skin. It takes a minute or so to control my breathing, which has raced ahead of itself. I can hear a helicopter spinning across the sky until it seems to be hovering right above the house. Maybe it's tracking a car thief or an escaped prisoner? What if he breaks into the house? A stern-looking policeman would appear on the news to warn members of the public not to approach this man, but what could I do? Laura would stumble in after midnight. She might even go straight to bed and it wouldn't be until the following morning that she'd discover my body.

My hearing is getting better, or is it just my imagination becoming more vivid? Every noise conjures up a new story. A roaring car engine, laughing children, dogs barking. I prefer it to the silence which torments me more than any fictitious murderer on the run. As quickly as the helicopter had appeared, it starts to fade away.

Laura is out with her friends from work. Laughing. Drinking. Flirting. I know I'm being silly but I remember the way I used to be. A few pints and an arm would be draped around an uneasy colleague, slurred words shouted into their ear above the music. Slobbered kisses, some offered, others stolen.

"Where are you off to tonight?" I'd asked earlier as she smoothed out the duvet across my chest.

"Some Italian restaurant that's meant to be great. Then we'll see where we end up."

"Who's all going?"

"Everyone from the office. Well, apart from Beccy. She couldn't get a babysitter."

"What about her husband?"

"They split up. Remember I told you."

"No."

"I did. It was ages ago."

She picked up the black dress, draping it over her head and letting it fall until it covered her body.

"You look nice," I mumbled.

"Thanks."

"New dress?"

"This thing? No, I got it ages ago. I wore it at Jim and Helen's twenty-fifth. Remember?"

"No."

"You're hopeless, Stephen," she laughed, leaning over and kissing my cheek. "You're always forgetting things these days. You'd forget your head if it wasn't screwed on... you know what I mean."

She buzzed in and out the room like an annoying fly that had sneaked into the house through a half-opened window. My eyes had followed her at first but they grew tired of the effort and I stared up at the artexed ceiling.

I did it myself. I had been so proud at the time. I was self-taught and though I wouldn't like to re-examine my earliest efforts, by the time it came to doing this ceiling, in what used to be the dining room, I was confident I could do a good job.

"That's me ready."

She stood at the foot of the bed and I nodded as I looked her up and down. She gave an appreciative smile and walked up to me, leaning over and kissing me. At one time she would have whispered "Don't wait up," but there was a hollow ring to the words now and she knew better than to even say them jokingly.

The house has been silent since the front door slammed shut. The television on the wall opposite stares down at me. I hadn't wanted Laura to turn it on, preferring to languish in my own martyred silence.

As soon as she'd gone, I was so desperate for *Coronation Street* to be on that I started crying.

The days are long and repetitive. I've lost any concept of time, save for the fact I know when it is light and when it is dark. I lie in bed, head propped up on two pillows, staring out the window. I watch the sunshine drift across the garden, warming the grass and coaxing it to grow. Leaves float from the trees, abandoning branches that swing naked in the wind. I like the rain best, when the clouds cast a dark shadow over the ground and spit out their contents. I close my eyes, soothed by the sound of the rain crashing off the glass.

I hear the bag filling up with liquid, a noise like water spilling out a broken gutter. I hate the thought of what is draped over the side of the bed and deliberately keeps it out of sight, though I can't keep it out of my mind.

I actually have impressive control over my bladder. Everyone says so. I've had more compliments than I care to remember. Sometimes it will be hours before I need to go. When I have the bag on I can last all night. It's neither a gift nor something to boast about but people seem to be impressed for some reason.

I can't believe I was so stupid as to insist the TV stayed off. The lack of a distraction is slowing down time so that each minute seems to take five to elapse. Mind you, when it's on I still grumble because it's stuck on the same channel. I have to choose whatever programme grabs my attention and hope that everything which follows isn't too bad.

When Laura is home, we sit together and stare at the screen. She scrolls through the channels every time the adverts come on, stopping at something that catches her eye and watching it for a few seconds before the screen changes again.

"Do you have to do that?" I say, gritting my teeth.

"What?"

"Just choose a channel and watch it."

"What's wrong with you?"

"Nothing."

Laura will make a face but the remote control is placed on the side of her chair and she sits, arms folded, eyes staring straight ahead. Invariably, we end up watching a programme about cars or houses that neither of us enjoys. It's a battle of wills. An old episode of *Only Fools And Horses* will come on, and I'll tell Laura to leave it. She'll sigh, throw the remote control down and go into the kitchen for a smoke at the back door.

That's at my insistence. I used to be a twenty-a-day man but four months lying flat on a bed in a Spanish hospital kicked the habit. I don't mind that she still smokes. I just don't want to see her or the trail of smoke that drifts across the room like a ghost from a *Scooby Doo* cartoon. If someone visits, Laura's dad or one of her friends, they'll have a cigarette with their coffee, sometimes conducting conversations as if I'm invisible. I breathe in deeply then, letting the traces of nicotine float into my mouth and tickle my throat, evoking memories I wish I could erase.

I tried smoking. Just the once. About a week after I finally got home from hospital. Laura held the cigarette, placing it between my lips so that I could inhale, but after a few draws my head began to spin, my stomach churned and I threw up all over my clothes.

She'll be smoking now with all her friends from

work, people I've never met but whose names I know, standing outside with a glass of white wine in one hand and a cigarette in the other as the waiters clear the table. Maybe she's at a pub? Someone will squeeze past her, placing his hands on her hips, pressing against her and whispering 'Excuse me'. She'll laugh and give him a smile and he'll go to the toilet thinking he's in with a chance. Bastard.

Suddenly I want to hear her voice even though, more often than not, we have nothing to say to each other. We still talk. Well, words come out that I recognise, but they're cold. Empty. We never speak about how we feel. For one thing I don't know. I'm not sure I can feel anything anymore.

I glance towards the window but the curtains hide the darkness that surrounds the house. I sigh and close my eyes, praying for a sleep that will never end.

The front door creaks. I hear it and open my eyes. Then it closes and footsteps creep up the stairs. I glance at the clock on the wall. Half past four. I spy the dawn trying to push its way through the gap in the curtains.

Laura laughs. It seeps through the floorboards above me and floats round the room like a ghoul. That sound used to send my stomach into spasms and a broad grin would always break out across my face. Now it only makes me shiver.

I hear her coming back downstairs and I wait until she's reached the bottom before I shut my eyes. She's standing at the door. Her breathing is calm, regular, soft. I picture her still wearing the black dress. I guess she's taken her shoes off. Where are they? Discarded in the hall or thrown across the bedroom floor? I breathe in deeply like I'm in a heavy sleep and I can smell her, perfume laced with whisky and wearing a stale cloak of nicotine. I feel her warm breath caress my cheek as she leans over the bed and rests her lips on my flesh. I hope she hadn't left a lipstick mark. There's no way I can wipe it off.

She slips away, heading back upstairs and I open my eyes again. I know I won't get back to sleep now. It's just a matter of counting the seconds 'til I think it's a reasonable time to wake Laura up. I reckon I can last until half past seven.

There's movement upstairs. I can hear her voice and another, deeper one. It's probably just the television, but what if it isn't? The bed creaks. She's getting comfortable. It creaks again. I hear everything at night. It is a noisy house that seems to stretch and groan in the dark as if it's relaxing after a long day tensed up in order that it doesn't fall down. There is more laughter, only some of which I recognise, as the bed creaks again, and I crunch my teeth together, trying to drown it out. I look down at my own body and see the bulge appear between my legs. There's nothing I can do to prevent it.

I close my eyes tightly as a tear of self-loathing escapes and races down my cheek. I picture the swimming pool. I stand at the edge and stare at the clear blue water. I push my feet closer to the edge until my toes caress the water. It feels cool. Soothing. I tense as I spring forward, my long, straight body piercing the smooth surface. I keep plunging downwards, my eyes looking for the bottom but it doesn't come as I push myself further into the hidden depths until I can't hear anything above me.

The Chauffeur

The door opens and an icy wind slaps her hard across the face. She looks away and starts the engine as he pours himself into the seat. The door slams shut. He burps and the smell of whisky and beer fills the car. She feels sick. She opens her window slightly and glances in the wing mirror, waiting for an opportunity to pull out from the kerb. He burps again. The car glides out but almost immediately halts at a red light. Slipping the gear into neutral she pulls on the handbrake, knocking his arm as he struggles with his seatbelt. She sighs and grabs it off him, clicking it into place. He farts. One. Two. Three. Like the cannon atop Edinburgh Castle heralding a new year. She rolls down the window as far as it goes, shivering. She knows she can suffer the cold for five minutes until they get home. Anything but the smell.

The lights change to green and the car is on the move, its headlights bearing into the back of the van in front like two giant spotlights trained on the lead singer of a band as he performs a ballad. The words 'Wash Me' are scrawled on its back door.

"What's all that shite? Turn it over. Pile of pish." He presses a button on the radio and the voices vanish into the night. "That's better."

Music fills the car. She doesn't recognise the song. It's loud and the singer is straining every sinew in his body to get the words out. It doesn't do him any good. He sounds awful.

"Anything to eat in the house? I'm fuckin'

starving." His head is bobbing back and forth as if he's lost control of his neck muscles. "What did you have for dinner?"

"Macaroni."

He grunts. She stares straight ahead as one song fades into another unfamiliar tune. The wind nips her cheek, a painful reminder that she's not just stuck in a bad dream.

"What about a sausage supper? Stop off at the chippy."

"But we're nearly home."

"Fuck's sake, Frances. I need real food. I'm not eating some macaroni shite. I want a chippy. Five minutes. It's only round the corner."

She wants to go home. No, she wants to stop the car, kick him out, reverse and then put her foot down hard on the accelerator and drive right over him, again and again until his fat, drunken, smelly body is flattened into the tarmac.

"Come on, darling. The chippy. For me. You can have some of my chips. Please."

He leans over and plants his wet lips on her cheek. It feels as if he's trying to suck the flesh off. His breath washes over her face and she swallows hard. They pass the turn-off for home and carry on down the road.

"That's my girl," he says, patting her leg. He slips his hand under her skirt and his fingers crawl up her thigh.

"Brian! I'm driving."

He ignores her. She thinks of slapping his arm away but is glad to see the chip shop come into view. He wouldn't have taken kindly to her resistance.

It was half past ten when she parked the car across

the road from the pub. Brian doesn't know she has started arriving early each night, happy to spend an extra fifteen or twenty minutes of blissful solitary confinement. No television. No blaring music. Or temperamental teenagers. And no drunken husband. Just her and the voices on the radio. Sad people telling sad stories to a silky voice at the other end of a telephone who dispenses perfunctory advice to them and the millions who listen in sympathetic silence. An agony aunt for the airwaves.

She discovered the station by accident one night as she waited. Earlier she had collected Caitlin from a friend's and her daughter had left the radio blasting out loud and messy music that made her head hurt. As the pub began to spew out its regulars in dribs and drabs she pressed buttons at random and then she heard the voice. A soft, fearful sound, which told of an abusive stepfather and a mother who didn't know or wouldn't see. She listened, captivated by the tale of ever increasing horror, only dragged back into her own sad story when the car door opened and Brian fell into the passenger seat.

After that, she made sure to tune in every night, a furtive listener for those few precious minutes. It was her secret, a place where she found people worse off than her; people – well, some of them – who had come out the other end of the tunnel and into the light. It didn't take her long to realise that the earlier she arrived outside the pub the more she could listen to the show.

She stored up the stories, committing many of them to memory. Women whose husbands left for someone younger; teenage girls pregnant and too scared to tell their parents; helpless drunks; hopeless romantics; marital punchbags. All form of human misery was broadcast into the night. Sometimes the stories made her laugh. Or cry. A few made her feel better about herself. Many made her feel worse, but she treasured every one.

Then one night she heard herself, like an echo through the airwaves. It was her story. Her life. The woman – her name was Eileen – told her story slowly, nervously, but Frances recognised every word as her own.

'I met my husband when I was fifteen,' Eileen said.

'Don't be nervous, love,' the presenter re-assured her.

'Okay, sorry … Well, we were at school together. We started going out and everything was fine. We both left school. I started university and he began working. Then, when I was eighteen I got pregnant. It was a total shock. We were still young. I had to drop out of uni to have the baby but my boyfriend was working and we thought we could manage. My parents were upset and a bit disappointed. So we got married. It made them feel a bit better. About a month after the wedding my daughter was born and everything was fine. I had my baby. We had a flat. And he had a job. The university said that I could go back the next year once my daughter was a few months old so I was still trying to do some studying at home, just to keep my mind active.

'Then, when she was about six-months-old, I found out I was pregnant again. I was devastated. I loved my daughter, don't get me wrong, but I didn't want another baby. My husband was really shocked. He couldn't believe it. Blamed me. And he started staying late at work, or going to the pub and coming home late. Drunk. Everything was a mess. I was a mess. My mum was helping me with the baby but I just felt I couldn't cope. I knew I wouldn't be able to go back to university now, once the second one came along, and I kind of just let myself go. I didn't care what I looked like. My hair was a mess. I never bothered putting any make-up on. I was fat. Then the baby was born – another daughter – and it made me pull myself together. I don't know why, but I just thought of these two wee helpless people and I realised it was my responsibility.

'My husband never really saw it like that. He stayed away from the house even more, drinking just about every night. He'd come home and start arguing. Shouting about being trapped in a house full of women. He was never violent to me. Never hit me. But he'd shout at me. The way I looked. The clothes I wore. The state of the house. But I had my daughters and I thought – it's stupid, I know – but I thought it was better to stick together, for better, for worse, you know. And my children needed a father as well. Then one day I looked in the mirror and I was thirty-six-years-old and I realised what a fool I'd been. My daughters are grown up now. One's nineteen and the other eighteen. They've both left home. They're at university. I'm so proud of them, doing what I should have done.

'My husband still went out every night to the pub. I knew he had other women. I'm not stupid. Don't ask me why I stayed all these years. I've no idea. I used to think I was quite clever – I was at university –

but that was the stupidest thing I've ever done. I looked in the mirror and my face was old and tired but I was only thirty-six and I knew I had to do something. I wanted my life back.

'So one night, when he was at the pub, I packed my clothes into a suitcase, jumped in the car and drove away. Just left him. I didn't know where I was going or what I was going to do. I just drove. That was two years ago. I've got a flat now. A job. And I'm planning to go back to university this year. Don't get me wrong. It was hard at first. Really hard. It was the first time I'd been on my own for about twenty years but it's been worth it. I can look it the mirror now and I like what I see.'

Tears run down Frances's cheeks as she remembers that voice, streams of sadness that she can't halt. She looks in the rear-view mirror and a blurred face stares back at her. She doesn't recognise the woman and that only makes her cry even harder. She can't just run off. Sarah's away, working down in London but Caitlin's still at school. She can't leave her but she can't take her. Eileen made it all sound so easy. Just pack up and drive away, not knowing where she was going but sure what she wanted to leave behind. It sounded great. Too good to be true.

In her head, Frances could do it. She can picture her flat. The furniture. The colour of the carpets. The vase of flowers on the window-sill. She'd sleep until noon. Eat lunch with the sun framing her at the table. Leave dirty dishes in the sink. Ignore the unmade bed until she curled back under the covers at night. And no waiting outside pubs.

The car door opens and Frances jumps. Brian heaves himself into the seat while she hides her face and wipes the tears away. The engine starts and she steers the car forward, heading home, the smell of chips drenched in vinegar filling up the confined space.

"Are you listening to that shite again? Turn it over. Bunch of sad bastards."

He presses a button on the radio and the voices vanish once more into the night. She catches her eye in the mirror. Just one more year, she thinks. One more year and Caitlin will have left for university. One more year and then she'll go. Just pack up and drive into the night. Brian burps. She grips the steering wheel. She wants to look in a mirror and like what she sees. One more year. He burps again.

Hungry Like The Wolf

L et's go to the seaside," Mandy suggested one night when we were standing in the doorway of an office. It was raining and I was soaked enough already without making it worse.

"The seaside?" I said.

"Aye."

"You're joking?"

"No."

"The seaside?"

"It'll be great, Michelle. A day out, away from here. Just the two of us."

"I don't know."

"Come on. It'll be a laugh."

"I've not been to the seaside for years."

We used to go when we were younger. Down to Ayr for the day. Getting the train from Central Station, me and Ellie sitting opposite each other so that we both got a window seat. Pressing our heads against the cold glass and watching the houses and the cars and buses and people flashing by while my mum sat and read *Hello* magazine.

Then we were out in the country, which was the best bit. The trees and the fields and the hills were bright green like we had been transported to some magical kingdom that we'd only ever dreamt of or read about in books. And sometimes, right in the middle of all that green, there would be one square of sunshine yellow. That was the field I wanted to be in, running about or lying on my back staring up at the blue sky. I loved looking at them out my window just for a few seconds. Then they were gone. We saw cows and sheep, just standing about and eating the grass. Chilling out. What a life. Sometimes the cows would be sitting down.

"Do you think they're having a rest?" Ellie asked and my mum smiled.

"No, darling. They're waiting for the rain."

We looked at her, puzzled.

"Cows can sense when it's going to rain. They're clever like that, so they're sitting down to make sure they get a dry bit of grass."

My mum knew everything about everything. At least I thought she did when I was younger.

We passed through places I'd never heard of like Johnstone and Howwood, and stopped at stations with names I thought were just made up. Milliken Park. Fairlie. Barassie. And when we got near Ayr, we'd both let out a big scream, which startled my mum and made other passengers stare at us, because we saw the sea. The water seemed to stretch for miles, and when it was sunny it glistened like God had sprinkled glitter over it.

It was freezing when we ran into it, though. That was always the first thing we did. Head straight from the station down to the beach. My mum would still be struggling across the sand as we raced to the water in our swimming costumes, a bundle of clothes and shoes abandoned in our wake.

My mum would shout 'Be careful you two,' but her words just sailed out to sea as we reached the water's edge and kept going 'til it was up to our knees. Sometimes it felt like the water was biting our legs but we just kept running about until the cold didn't bother us. My mum sat down beside our clothes and watched us, though most of the time her head was buried in her magazine. I was there and I was older, so she knew Ellie would be safe.

We'd be in the water for ages, hours sometimes. My mum had sandwiches in her bag for when we got hungry, corned beef or cheese and tomato, with a plastic bottle of Irn Bru to drink. The food was stuffed in our mouths while my mum told us to take our time. It always tasted salty because we didn't wash our hands first but we didn't care. Then it was back into the water.

If it got too cold, usually on days when it was cloudy and windy, we'd get changed and head back up to the shops. Ellie and I would be looking out for a cafe to get ice-cream. If my mum was in a good mood she'd get us a ninety-nine each, otherwise we had to make do with a wee cone.

"I'm not made of money," she'd say when we started moaning and we knew not to say anything else. The ice-cream still tasted brilliant, much better than the stuff from the van back home.

Sometimes there would be a fairground but we usually just went to the swing park because it didn't cost anything. I could see all the rides from the top of the shute. They looked brilliant and everybody seemed to be having a great time. I wished we had money to go on them. I dreamt of finding a ten-pound note lying on the ground and spending it all on rides for me and Ellie while my mum watched us, drinking a cup of tea I bought her with the money.

At the end of the day, when it was time to get the train back home, I was glad my mum hadn't wasted her money on daft rides. We'd go to the chippy across the road from the station and she would buy a fish supper, a sausage supper and three cans of Irn Bru.

Ellie and I shared the sausage supper. They always gave you two sausages so we could have one each and there were loads of chips as well. We always timed it so that we bought them just before the train left and we sat eating as it pulled out of the station, the smell filling the carriage. I could see people looking at us, jealous and probably wishing they'd done the same thing. It was the perfect end to a perfect day.

Mandy and I had arranged to meet at ten o'clock inside Central Station, right beside the Starbucks. I got a number forty-three into town and the rain battered off the bus all the way in. I could hardly see anything out the windows. It hadn't stopped raining for days, and I'd got soaked again last night. I could feel my nose running and I tried to sniff it away. I looked round to make sure nobody was watching me and then wiped my nose on my sleeve.

I'd finished working early so that I could get some sleep and I prayed for a sunny day when I got into bed. I didn't see Mandy before I got a taxi home. She'd gone off in a white car and I couldn't be bothered waiting for her to come back. I still had the car registration number in my bag, though.

She was already there when I walked up to the shop, drinking a cup of coffee and smoking a cigarette.

"You look like shit," I said, giving her a hug. "Have you not been to bed?"

"I've not even been home."

I looked at her and noticed she was still wearing the same clothes from the night before.

"Where were you?"

"At some posh house. I don't know where it was."

"The guy with the white motor?"

"Aye. It was alright. He wasn't a psycho or anything… Here, I got you a present."

She opened her bag and pulled out a bottle of perfume. Chanel No.5.

"It smells nice," she said. "Give me your hand."

I held it out and she sprayed some on my wrist. I rubbed my other wrist against it and held it up to my nose.

"That's alright. Do you not want it?"

"I got some as well," she said, "and this too." She held out a black dress. It looked really classy. Expensive. "I got knickers and a bra to go with it."

"You're like Mary fuckin' Poppins with that bag. What else have you got in there?"

"Just a few things. Well, what was I supposed to do, Michelle. He went for a shower. I mean, he was asking for it."

I just shook my head and handed her the perfume back.

"Keep that in your bag for me," I said. "Come on, we don't want to miss the train."

As the train pulled out of the station, I pressed my head against the glass, wanting to recapture something, I don't know, being a wee girl again maybe. It didn't work, though. The window was splattered with rain and Mandy kept talking, distracting me.

It was quiet on the train, not like the way I

remembered it when I was younger. An older woman and her husband sat side by side, not talking. Behind them a young guy leant against the window listening to his iPod. I tried guessing what the song was. He looked like a student but I didn't have a clue what they liked. I realised I didn't know anything about music. Ellie would know. Maybe she was listening to the same stuff. I was tempted to ask the guy but I didn't have the guts.

The ticket collector came through the doors at the end of the carriage and stopped at a woman sitting with a pram. I guessed it was a baby girl because of the pink cover hanging over the side. Mandy saw me staring and looked round.

"I'll sort out the tickets," she said with a wink. She pulled her skirt up until most of her legs were on show. I sighed.

The guy was getting closer. He had to nudge the student who looked as if he was sleeping and then he came to us. Mandy looked up and smiled, opening her legs a bit. I reached over and handed the guy the tickets, which he took even though he kept staring at Mandy's legs. She looked at me when he moved away.

"What?" I said.

"You bought tickets?"

"Yes."

"When?"

"At the station, before I met you."

"What for?"

"Because you need tickets for the train."

"What a waste of money. You needn't think I'm paying for them."

"Don't worry. I don't want your money."

Mandy would sometimes get the train to visit her

mum in Falkirk. She didn't always have enough money so she'd give the ticket collector a blow job in the toilet so he wouldn't throw her off. But I wanted today to be normal. Just two pals going to the seaside for a day out.

It was still raining when we got to Ayr, even heavier than it had been in Glasgow. We stood just inside the front door of the station and stared out. There was hardly anybody about. Mandy handed me a cigarette and we both blew smoke out into the rain.

"This is fuckin' shite," she said as she flicked her cigarette into a puddle where it drowned right away. "There'll be nothing to do here. We can't even go down the beach."

"Why not?"

"Are you blind or something, Michelle? Look at the rain. We'd be soaked by the time we get across the road. What a shite fuckin' day."

She was right. This place was dead in the rain. There would be no beach and no water and no swing park and no rides at the fairground. We'd be as well getting something out the chippy now and then catch the next train home. I started laughing. Mandy stared at me like I was crazy but I kept laughing.

"What's so funny?" she said.

"This," I said, pointing out at the rain. "Come on, Mandy, you have to laugh. Look at it. A day at the seaside? You get better weather on the streets."

"But I was looking forward to today."

"So was I."

"Just for a wee change. Away from everything. But this is pure shite, so it is."

Mandy wasn't happy. Neither was I but there was nothing we could do about it so there was no point sulking.

"Come on," I said, taking her arm.

"I'm not going out in that."

"We're here now, Mandy. Come on, we'll go and get a cup a tea and something to eat in that wee café over there."

Mandy shook her head but she let me lead her out into the rain. It was like we'd stopped under a waterfall. We were both soaked in seconds. I thought I'd dressed sensibly with a pair of jeans on but they'd turned all dark and were sticking to my legs. Mandy had a denim mini skirt on with just a t-shirt under her jacket. The water was running down her legs like she'd wet herself. Her hair was a mess, flat on her head with straggly bits sticking to her cheeks. I knew mine would be just as bad.

It didn't matter that we ran as fast as we could – which wasn't very fast – all the way to the café, not even bothering to stop at the side of the road as a taxi drove towards us. We still got soaked. The taxi driver slammed his brakes on and I heard his horn. I don't even know if we'd have been that bothered if he'd hit us.

The woman behind the counter gasped when she saw us and was right over in a flash, pulling us towards the table nearest her till.

"You'll get a heat from the kitchen," she said, almost pushing us down into the seats. "It's not great but it might dry you off a bit. What a day. Here, give me your jackets."

We looked at each other, suspecting it would be the last we'd ever see of them. It wasn't our fault we thought like that. We'd both learned that you couldn't trust anybody.

"Come on, give me your jackets. I'll hang them up through the back beside the fire. You don't want to catch your death, do you?"

I shook my head as I struggled to tug my jacket off. It was heavy with the rain and the woman had to give me a hand to get my arm out of one of the sleeves. I shivered when I sat there without it.

"Wait and I'll see if I've got anything for you," the woman said, shaking her head. I looked at Mandy and she was shaking as well. I tried to force a smile but my teeth kept clattering together. Mandy sort of smiled but she kept blowing with her bottom lip sticking out to stop the raindrops running down her face.

"Come on through here a minute," the woman said, nodding her head backwards through the doorway she stood at. Neither of us moved at first but she said it again, almost ordering us and we got up and shuffled through behind her.

It was a small sitting room, with two armchairs, a table in between them and a television in one corner, a three-bar electric fire in the other. There was a faint glow from the bars, like they were either waking up or dying. The chairs looked old, with chunks out of the seats. On the table was a *Daily Record* and an ashtray that was almost overflowing with cigarette ends.

"I've got a couple of overalls you can put on just now if you want, just 'til your clothes get dried a bit." The woman dropped them on to one of the chairs. They had a flowery pattern and I could see Mandy looking at them as if to say, I'm not wearing that, but I smiled at the woman.

"Thanks," I whispered.

"Now, you need to get those wet clothes off. I'll get a chair and you can put them over it in front of the fire. What a day for being out. You girls must be mad."

She disappeared back through to the front of the café and I unbuttoned my jeans and started trying to take them off. It was harder than I thought since they were soaking but I kept pushing them until they were down past my knees.

"What are you doing?" Mandy said.

"Getting my wet stuff off."

"Are you kidding? You're not putting that thing on, are you?"

"How not?"

"Fuck's sake, Michelle. Who is this woman anyway? We don't have a clue who she is and here's you stripping down to your knickers in the back of her shop. What if she's some sort of weirdo that's into young girls."

"Shut up, Mandy and don't be daft. She's like a mum, or a granny,"

"She's not like my mum."

"You mean she's not drunk ... Sorry, Mandy. I didn't mean that."

She turned her back on me and I stepped out of my jeans, leaving them on the floor. I didn't mean to say that about Mandy's mum. She was an alcoholic. Mandy had told me. That's why Mandy ended up in care. But I shouldn't have said anything. She could say loads of stuff back at me if she wanted to. I pulled my t-shirt off and took one of the flowery overalls. My knickers and bra were wet as well but I wasn't taking them off.

"What are you doing," the woman said, coming into the room as I started to put the overall on. "Here, give yourself a wee dry with this." She threw a towel at me and I caught it. It wasn't big but I was still able to rub myself a bit with it. It was my hair I wanted to dry most. The towel was soaking after a minute but I didn't care.

"Are you not getting out of your wet clothes?" the woman asked Mandy who still stood with her back to me. She shrugged.

"Well, it's up to you, love, but it's not good for you to stay in those clothes."

The woman had scooped up my stuff and started hanging it on the chair she'd brought in. I'd put the overall on and the woman smiled.

"You look grand. Sit yourself down and I'll get you a wee cup of tea."

When she was gone again, Mandy started taking her clothes off. She still wouldn't look at me. I decided not to say anything, just let her calm down a bit. She had to use the same towel as me but she didn't moan about it being wet. I watched her as she got dried. There was a massive bruise on her back and a red line that snaked across from her right shoulder to her left hip. I didn't want to think what had caused that.

"What are you looking at?" Mandy said, standing in her underwear with her hands on her hips.

"Eh … Nothing … Nothing."

"Aye, well, just as well," she said, snatching the other overall and stepping into it.

"I'm sorry, Mandy."

"Forget it."

"I didn't mean to say it."

"Well, it's true."

"But I shouldn't have said anything."

She shook her head and sat down in the other seat. I noticed she didn't lean back but perched herself on the edge. Part of me wanted to ask about her back but my big mouth had caused enough problems already. Maybe later.

The woman's name was Agnes. She brought us mugs of boiling hot tea and a couple of bacon rolls each. It was magic. We stuffed the rolls down but had to sip the tea. I put my face over the mug and blew into it, letting the heat blast up on to my cheeks. Agnes watched us while we ate and drank with a big smile on her face. She'd locked up the café so she could sit in the back with us. Nobody'll be out today, she told us as she sat down on another chair she'd brought through. Well, we were out, I thought of saying to her but it sounded cheeky in my head and I didn't want to annoy her.

"You remind me of my daughter," Agnes said. I knew she had been staring at me for ages and I didn't want to look up and catch her eye. I forced a smiled.

"Same brown hair, blue eyes. You're a bonny-looking lassie, Michelle."

"Thanks."

I didn't know what else to say, apart from 'Are you blind?' I knew I wasn't pretty. Not now. Maybe I had been. Once. You'd have to ask someone else that, though. Not my mum, since she would be biased, but somebody else who remembered me before all the drugs and everything came along. It still felt nice, though, somebody saying you were pretty. Bonny-looking. I liked the sound of that.

"What's your daughter called?" Mandy asked.

"Jacqueline."

"What age is she?"

"She's dead."

I almost dropped my mug. Agnes shook her head.

"She would be nineteen now. Twenty seventh of August was her birthday."

"What happened?" My question was a croak.

"She was knocked down on her way home from school," Agnes said, shaking her head. "She was only twelve. In first-year at high school. Just stepped out from behind the school bus ... You never know the minute."

I expected Agnes to burst into tears but she didn't, just stared at the fire like she could see her daughter before her, in the glow of the bars. I wished I could have gone over to her and given her a cuddle. It wouldn't make things better, but I knew it was the right thing to do, after her being really nice to us. But I didn't move. Maybe it was because Mandy was here and she might have slagged me later or maybe it was just because I was scared myself. Maybe that one cuddle would make Agnes cry – and me too?

"I'm sorry," I said to break up the silence.

"Thanks, love. You're a good girl," she said, patting my knee. "Your mum's lucky to have you."

If only Agnes knew. I wasn't telling her, though. It was better to keep some things to myself. I didn't want to disappoint her, not when she was being so nice, and it might have made her sadder.

She told us her husband left her about two years after Jacqueline died. "He couldn't cope," she said. "She was a real daddy's girl and it broke his heart when she died."

She didn't know where he was. Just walked out the house one day and never came back. He left a note, she told us, which said *'I'm leaving. The sadness is killing me. Love, Denis.'*

I could feel a few tears filling up my eyes when she was speaking. It was the saddest story in the world. I took her hand and held it gently. I could see Mandy frowning and knew she would say something later but I didn't care. She went through to the front to get more tea as Agnes kept talking, telling me how she had kept running the café, even after Denis left.

"I think he's dead too," she whispered to me. "I just think he couldn't live without his wee girl."

"But what about you? Why did he leave you?"

"I wasn't enough. I don't blame him, love. If you ever have any kids of your own, you'll know what I'm talking about. Ask your mum. She'll tell you."

The rain didn't go off all day. We stayed in the back of Agnes's café 'til about two o'clock. Our clothes weren't completely dry but they would have to do. She made us macaroni and chips for lunch so I didn't feel like a chippy before we left. I wasn't bothered. It hadn't really been a day like the ones I had when I was younger.

Agnes let us out the shop with a big hug. Mandy almost shrugged her off but I kept hold of her. It felt nice.

"You look after yourself, love," she said, giving me a kiss on my cheek.

"Thanks, Agnes."

"And remember, next time you're in Ayr, pop in and say hello."

"I will."

"Promise?"

"I promise."

She gave me another hug.

"Come on, Michelle. We're going miss the train," Mandy shouted as she started to cross the road. She never bothered saying thanks to Agnes but there was nothing I could do about that. Agnes stood at the door of the café, waving to us 'til we disappeared inside the station.

The train had just pulled out of Ayr when Mandy pushed a bundle of notes across the table.

"What's that?" I said.

"What do you think it is? Your share."

I lifted the money and counted it. Ninety quid. Jesus! How many punters would I have to go with to get that sort of money? I frowned at Mandy.

"What?" She said.

I shook my head.

"What's your problem?"

"Tell me you didn't rob Agnes."

Mandy shrugged.

"You're a fuckin' cunt, so you are."

"Who are you calling a cunt?"

"You. Fuckin' cunt." I stood up and threw the money at her. The notes – tenners and twenties – floated about the carriage and Mandy scrambled to get them all. Two women sitting a couple of seats behind us were staring but they turned away when I stared back.

"What's up with you? Ninety quid. Are you loaded or something that you don't need it?"

"You're a cunt."

"Don't call me that again, Michelle."

Mandy had got all the money and she held it out. A peace offering. I spat in her face.

"She was nice to us. Gave us food and dried our clothes and all you could do was rob her."

Mandy stuffed the money into her pocket and glanced away like she wasn't bothered but then spun round and punched me. Her first slammed into my cheek and I fell back. I bounced up like the seat was a trampoline and took a swing at her but she managed to dodge it.

"You disgust me, you fuckin' wee cunt," I shouted and spat at her again. It hit her jacket but she never even looked, just smiled at me.

"I've got one hundred and eighty quid. So I'm a fuckin' rich wee cunt."

I stormed away up the carriage, shouting "What the fuck are you looking at?" into the faces of the two women. I kept walking until I was at the front of the train and I threw myself on to an empty seat.

"Are you alright, love?" An old guy with snow-white hair and a thin grey moustache leant over and asked. I hadn't realised I was crying.

"Fuck off and mind your own business," I said and he sat back.

Nobody bothered me after that, even though I kept crying, not even the ticket collector who waited patiently for a few minutes while I searched in my pockets. He never said anything when I handed him a soggy bit of paper that was my ticket.

I left Mandy's ticket in my pocket. Fuck her. She could suck the guy's dick if she wanted. I didn't care. She even had enough money to buy a ticket.

Last Chance On The Stairway

Fiona decided to leave me though I wouldn't have known if I hadn't met her coming down the tenement stairs as I was walking up to the flat.

"Where are you going?"

She looked at the suitcase in her hand and I did too, and then she shrugged.

"Are you going on holiday?" I asked. Maybe she'd told me and I'd forgotten about it.

"No, I'm leaving."

"You're leaving?"

"I'm leaving."

"You're leaving."

"Yes."

"Why are you leaving?"

Fiona sighed and I slumped against the stone wall.

It was like I was sixteen again and Jacqui McKenna was dumping me on the stairs between English and Chemistry.

'I don't understand,' I whined to Jacqui, who folded her arms across the first breasts I had ever touched. It had been the most intense three weeks of my life. I thought we were in love. Jacqui told me we weren't.

'But why?' I asked, feeling tears beginning to well up and hoping they wouldn't spill out, or that anyone else would notice as they passed us, otherwise my life would be over and I'd have to leave school and change my name and move to a different town.

'You're just … just…'

'I'm just what?' I asked, taking a step towards Jacqui and stumbling so that I fell at her feet.

'You're just not John Taylor,' Jacqui said.

'What?'

'You're just not John Taylor.'

'Who the fuck is John Taylor?'

'You don't know who John Taylor is?'

'Is he that guy in sixth year with the crooked nose?'

'No, he's the bass guitarist in Duran Duran, the really beautiful one.'

I looked up at her, still on my knees, as her eyes drifted beyond me and I glanced over my shoulder, half expecting to see John Taylor standing there. She turned and walked away, leaving me kneeling and watching her, straining to get one final glimpse up her skirt.

Fiona started to move down the stairs and I blocked her way, tempted to fall to my knees again like a broken-hearted teenager.

"I need to go, Paul," she said, bumping the case against my legs.

I stood aside so she could pass.

"I don't understand," I said. "Just give me a reason."

Fiona stopped and looked back up at me.

"I deserve that at least," I said.

"You want to know why I'm leaving?"

"Yes."

"You really want to know?"

"I need to know."

She shook her head and sighed again. "I'm just sick of you playing that bloody bass guitar all the time."

Violence of Summer (Love's Taking Over)

"Out you get, Biscuit."

Tommy's voice was gentle but definite. I sat for a few seconds and then sighed before climbing out. Tommy put his hands on my shoulders to stop me falling over. At either side of him stood Cliff and Frank, arms folded, faces impassive. Their eyes bore into me, waiting for any sudden bid for freedom, but I knew I wasn't going anywhere.

"Fag?"

"No, it's just the way I walk."

"You want a fag?" Tommy said, holding out a packet. I shrugged.

"Sorry," he said. "I forgot … Cliff, untie Biscuit so he can have a smoke."

I shook my hands to encourage the blood to flow back into them, and then put a cigarette in my mouth, leaning towards the match Tommy sheltered in his hands. I took a deep draw and then blew it out into the air. It was a cold night and I couldn't tell where the smoke stopped and my breath started.

I looked up at the black sky sparkling like a jeweller's tray. The full moon lit up the clearing where we stood. Tommy was smoking as well and we stood in silence while birds lurking in the trees sung a late-night lament.

Frank leant forward and whispered in Tommy's ear.

"Fuck's sake, Frank. Could you not have gone before we came?"

"I did but I need to go again."

"You're worse than a bloody kid."

"Sorry, Tommy. It's the cold."

"Well, hurry up. Malky'll be here soon."

Frank jogged over to the trees and disappeared behind a giant oak. A few seconds later, we could hear him. Tommy shook his head and flicked his cigarette on to the ground. I continued smoking mine until it was right down to the stub and every draw burnt my lips; I didn't know whether it would be my last one.

They had been waiting for me when I walked into the house. Tommy was in the kitchen having a cup of tea while Cliff and Frank were on the PlayStation in the living-room. I could hear them arguing. I thought of running but if I did it would be an admission of guilt and I hadn't been accused of anything yet. So I walked through to the kitchen, sat down beside Tommy, poured myself a cup of tea and lit a cigarette. Then he invited me to go for a drive.

"Is that you finished now?" Tommy asked Frank as he returned.

"Yes."

"You want another smoke, Biscuit?"

"Thanks."

"You should have enough time before he comes."

I had just started smoking when my mobile began ringing. Everyone stared at me. *We Wish You A Merry Christmas* filled the night air.

"What will I do?" I asked.

"I don't know," said Tommy.

"Will I answer it?"

"No."

"No?"

"Yes."

"No?"

"Answer it."

"You want me to answer it?"

"Answer the fuckin' phone."

I took the phone out my jacket pocket.

"Hello? … It's for you," I said, holding the mobile out to Tommy.

"For me?"

He took the phone as I mouthed, "It's Malky" and he suddenly looked tense. He walked over to the van and got inside. Cliff and Frank didn't take their eyes off me but I watched Tommy. Every now and then he would glance over with a look that was measuring me for the drop. My eyes searched for any sign of escape but the only way was the dirt track that we'd driven up. They would catch me within minutes if I didn't run into Malky coming along the road first. There was nothing else to do but finish the cigarette.

Tommy slammed the van door and walked over, handing me the phone. I slipped it into my pocket.

"He'll be here in five minutes," he muttered. He shuffled back to the van and leant against the bonnet with arms folded.

I liked Tommy. He had a tough-guy exterior but was a big pussycat underneath. Well, maybe not a pussycat, more a sort of friendly lion, though he would still bite your head off if you pulled his tail. In the van, he'd kept glancing at me and muttering, "Biscuit, Biscuit," with a shake of his head.

"Nights are fair drawing in," I said, but Cliff and Frank remained stony-faced. I could hear a car approaching and looked round to see a set of headlights painting the road blue silver. It was Malky. Tommy spotted the car and sprang up, coming over and standing beside us. The car stopped a few yards away, its lights holding us in its beam. The engine was killed but no-one got out. I tried staring through the light to see who was inside but it was impossible. I knew Malky was there but I didn't know who'd been driving. That was normally Tommy's job.

Somebody dropped one, which sounded louder in the silent night.

"Was that you?" Tommy asked Frank.

"What?"

"Did you fart?"

"No!"

"Did you?"

No!" said Cliff.

"Well somebody did, and there are only three of us here."

"Four."

"Well, it wasn't Biscuit."

"How do you know?"

"Because I'm standing right next to him."

The headlights snapped off and the car doors opened. It was suddenly much darker than it had been before, even with the moon hovering above.

"Hello Biscuit," a throaty voice said as the figures reached us.

"Malky."

"It's a nice night for it, don't you think?"

"Absolutely."

Tommy stepped forward. "Everything's ready."

"First class."

Malky shuffled up to me 'til I could smell his garlic breath.

"You know why you're here, Biscuit?"

I shrugged.

"Maybe you do and maybe you don't, but I'll tell you just so that it's crystal clear."

Another fart blasted out into the air. Malky glanced past me with a look that could suck the life out of you.

"Was that you?" he snapped at Frank.

"Sorry, Malky. I had a Chinese earlier on. Sweet and sour. It's playing havoc with my guts."

Malky shook his head. "Do that again and I'll cut off your nose and stick it up your arse."

Frank nodded and I allowed myself a smile.

"Something funny, Biscuit?"

"No, Malky."

"Good, because there is nothing funny about your situation. Nothing funny at all."

My only hope was that it would be quick. I knew what they could do and I wasn't very good with pain. As my eyes adjusted to the dark again, I noticed the guy standing behind Malky. He wore a long black leather coat and his hands were clasped together in front of him like he was praying. I didn't recognise him, which made me think he was the one who would do the dirty deed. The shades were a bit ridiculous, though. Maybe he was blind?

"Look Malky, I'm sorry," I said.

"You're sorry?"

"I shouldn't have taken the money."

"Biscuit, Biscuit," he said, slapping my face gently. "It's not about the money."

"It's not?"

He nodded towards Stevie Wonder who strode back to the car. He opened the back door and leant inside, pulling someone out. They walked towards us, the other figure stumbling at Stevie's rough prompting. When they reached us I realised it was Linda. She looked up and I knew when our eyes met that there would be no mercy in this place tonight.

"Biscuit, I believe you've met my wife before."

"Eh, yes. Hi."

"Don't be so shy, Biscuit. Give her a wee kiss."

"A kiss?"

"You don't want to kiss my wife? ... No? Okay, so let me get this clear, Biscuit. You don't mind shoving your cock into my wife but you don't want to give her a friendly wee peck on the cheek? That doesn't seem right to me. Does that seem right to you, Tommy?"

"No, Malky."

"It doesn't seem right to me," said Cliff.

"Who the fuck asked you?" snapped Malky.

"Look, Malky," I said. "I'm sorry."

He looked at me and shook his head. "Save your breath, Biscuit, you'll need it ... Have you got it?" he asked Tommy.

"It's in the van."

"And everything's ready?"

Tommy nodded. "Through there," he said, pointing towards a set of trees. He nudged Cliff and Frank and the two of them headed over to the van.

"Walk with me, Biscuit. Tommy'll lead the way."

Malky and I followed Tommy towards the trees with Stevie Wonder and Linda behind. I could hear puffing and panting from the van but I didn't dare look round.

"You know, Biscuit. I always liked you," said Malky. "I don't know what it was about you but I thought you were alright. You pissed me off when you stole the money but I might have been able to forgive that... Who am I kidding? I would have shot you through the head for that, but this? What were you thinking about, Biscuit? Did you really think that I wouldn't find out? ... Well, did you?"

"Sorry, Malky ... Yes."

He laughed and slapped my back with force as if I had a piece of food stuck in my throat.

"You always did have a weird sense of humour, Biscuit."

We emerged into another clearing and stopped before a hole in the ground. Cliff and Frank appeared, carrying a big wooden box they manoeuvred past us and slid into the hole.

"Take the fuckin' lid off first," Tommy said. The two of them lay down at either side of the hole and leant over the edge, the top halves of their bodies disappearing from view as they wrestled with the lid. They managed to force it up once before it slipped out of their grasp and slammed back down on the box.

"Fuckin' hell, Tommy," said Malky. "Where did you get these Muppets from? Why don't we dig another hole for them while we're here?"

Tommy had to lie down and help them. Eventually, the lid was propped up safely against the side of the hole. I stared down at the box and I knew this was going to be my final resting place.

We lay side by side facing each other, Linda and I, but

making certain we didn't touch, not when Malky was standing over us.

"Hey, Tommy, why is Biscuit called Biscuit?"

"Don't know, Malky."

"Cause he goes to pieces in the box."

Malky started laughing so hard that I thought he was going to cough up a lung. Tommy joined in without enthusiasm.

"So long, farewell, auf wiedersehen, goodbye," Malky sang as the lid was lowered on top of us. In the complete and terrifying darkness, we clung to each other in the vain hope of finding some comfort. I could hear someone on top of us going from corner to corner screwing down the lid. When they'd finished they climbed out and the earth started to rain down like hailstones on a glass roof.

Linda gripped me even tighter, then let out a scream that scared the shit out of me. I didn't know what to do. It must have taken at least half an hour to fill the hole but eventually there was just silence. And darkness. Linda had stopped screaming, either too exhausted or terrified.

The last time we had lain together had been in my bed. Naked. Sweating. Satisfied. Now I felt as if I was going to wet myself.

"Linda?" I whispered. "Linda?"

"What?"

I didn't know what else to say. I moved my hand up until it touched her face, then I gently ran my fingers over her skin, caressing her cheeks, her nose, and her eyelids. When I stroked her lips, she opened them and as I slipped my finger inside her mouth, she snapped it shut.

"AAGH!"

She released my finger.

"This is all your fault!" she screamed.

"Mine?"

"Aye."

"That was bloody sore, Linda … How's it my fault?"

"Well, if you hadn't got me pregnant, Malky would never have found out."

"You're pregnant?"

"Yes."

"Could you not have just pretended it was his?"

"No."

"Why not?"

"Malky's not packing."

"What the hell does that mean?"

"Fuckin' hell, Biscuit. He fires blanks. He can't have children."

"Oh."

"Oh … is that all you can say?"

"Well …"

"When I got pregnant, I had to tell him."

"Could you not have got rid of it?"

"What, an abortion?"

"Yes."

"I'm a Catholic, Biscuit. It's against my religion."

"Against your religion?"

"Anyway, I always wanted a baby."

Maternal instinct, biological clocks and the Pope had well and truly buried me.

"Is it a boy or a girl?" I asked after a few minutes.

"I don't know. I wanted it to be a surprise."

She took my hand and guided it 'til it rested on her stomach.

"I can't feel anything," I said.

"I'm only just over three months. The books say it's later when it starts kicking and stuff."

"See if it's a boy, could you call it after me?"

"What, Biscuit? No chance."

"My real name's not Biscuit."

"What is it then?"

"Conor."

"So where did the Biscuit come from?"

"Conor McVitie."

"Conor's a nice name," she said, searching out my lips in the darkness and caressing them with her own. I felt the tears run down her cheeks.

"You'd make a great mum."

It was the wrong thing to say when I thought it was the nicest. Linda started howling again. It was the worst sound I had ever heard in my life. It seemed to go on and on, getting louder and more painful, though after a few minutes I swore I could hear her screaming Christmas tunes.

It took me a minute or so to realise what it was and I scrambled through every pocket. By the time I found it, the ringing had stopped, but so had Linda.

"You've got a phone?" she mumbled through the snot and the tears. "You've got a phone? YOU'VE GOT A PHONE!"

Now we were both laughing and kissing and cuddling. Everything was going to be alright. We were going to be saved. All of us. Me. Linda. And the baby.

"There's just one thing," I said when the excitement had started to simmer down.

"What?" Linda asked as she kissed me.

"Do you know where we are?"

The Reflex

Denis is staring out the window, cradling a cup of tea that must have long gone cold.

"What's your story then?" he asks.

"My story?"

He nods. "Everyone's got a story. What's yours?"

It's not the first time I've been asked. It seems to be the way of things in here. You tell me yours and I'll tell you mine. Hoping my story is worse than theirs, as if it's any consolation.

Denis takes a sip of tea and frowns but has another drink, a gulp this time. He's watching me, waiting, eager to hear what I've got to say. Desperate maybe?

"So it starts like any other day," I say with a smile. "I wake up with a hard-on that I barely notice, waiting for it to deflate before getting up to the toilet. Only this time it doesn't go down. Ten minutes come and go and I'm desperate to empty my bladder. It's no laughing matter. I have to sit down and push it under the seat but what a relief it is as I let it all out. I think about having a wank but only for a second. I'm never in the mood when I wake up."

"I know what you mean."

I look at Denis. He's at least seventy-five, if not older. Bald with skin like wizened prunes and a blotchy skull like Gorbachev. The top two buttons of his shirt are undone and a few grey chest hairs peek out shyly.

"What are you smiling about?" he asks.

"Nothing."

"Don't think an old man can still get it up, do you?"

"No, it's not that."

"Well, let me tell you I have no problems in that department. No problems at all."

He says it with defiant pride and I don't want to provoke him into proving it to me. I can't imagine someone that age still being interested.

"So you were saying?" Denis says.

"Well I go downstairs for a cigarette. I put the radio on and Duran Duran are singing Union of the Snake. I'm standing at the back door in a t-shirt and a pair of boxers and it's bloody Baltic."

It was Alison's idea to smoke at the back door. More of an ultimatum, actually. She wouldn't let Nicola stay in a smoky house. 'If you want to kill yourself that's up to you, Mark, but not your daughter,' she warned me in a tone I always wished she would leave behind in the classroom. Of course I did what she said. Anything to have Nicola. She stayed every weekend, either on a Friday or Saturday night as well as Wednesdays. That was my favourite time, eating dinner together, and then sitting while she flicked through all the music and kids' channels, neither of us saying much. It felt nice, like we were a normal family and her mum was out at work or upstairs washing her hair.

The next morning I'd wake her up, cajoling and coercing her to get out of bed. Making her breakfast, checking that everything was in her school bag. Giving her a pound for the tuck-shop. I loved driving her to school. I'd park in the street and we would walk to the gates, hand in hand. She always gave me a kiss and a cuddle, and then she was away to catch her friends as I shouted 'Have a nice day,' my words caught in the wind and blown out of earshot.

Weekends were different. I had to wrack my brain for things to do. Cinema, bowling, shopping, visiting my parents. I liked the cinema best. Dreaded going to see my mum and dad. My mum never said anything, not when Nicola was there, but I could tell from her disappointed eyes that this was not how she wanted her granddaughter to be brought up.

"That's grandparents for you," Denis says. "My wife was always giving me into trouble for sticking my nose in. 'They're not your kids,' she'd tell me. I knew that but sometimes … sometimes it's so hard."

"Are they badly behaved?"

"No, not at all. It's just … well, you have your own way of bringing kids up. You do your best, you know, but other people have different ideas, even your own kids, and they let theirs do things I wouldn't dream of allowing. They all just called me curmudgeonly and laughed at me."

"Curmudgeonly?"

"Aye, I had to look it up in the bloody dictionary."

Denis is lucky, though I don't tell him that. There is a constant stream of people visiting him. Sons, daughters, grandchildren, friends. Sometimes I watch enviously as they fuss over him. Denis loves the attention even though I can hear him protesting, telling everyone to leave him alone.

I get visitors, my mum and dad mostly. Phil tries to come once a week. We've been friends since school but I know it's hard for him, staring at me, remembering the way I used to look when I was fifteen, twenty, thirty, thirty-five. I'll be forty-two next birthday. Maybe. The same age your grandpa died, my dad tells me and I thank him for his words of comfort.

My brother calls me at the weekend, always at night. Well, it's the middle of the afternoon in Boston. We talk about football. Only football. He prefers it that way. He's two years older than me. He offers to fly over but I tell him not to bother. I'll visit him when I recover. You better, he tells me with a playful threat and we both laugh. The same laugh, like an echo down the phone.

Alison visits me every couple of weeks on her own. I don't want Nicola to come here. I see her whenever I'm allowed out for an afternoon. The old access rules don't apply any more. When I thank Alison for that she bursts into tears and I sit there helpless, wanting to wrap my arms round her and comfort her but not sure what boundaries still exist.

"I think I'll make a fresh cup of tea," Denis says, standing up and stretching.

"Sit yourself down. I'll get it for you,"

"Don't be daft. I need the exercise." He looks down at his mug, his mind debating whether he can reach over and get it. I stretch across and lift it up and he takes it with a grateful nod.

"Do you want one?" he asks.

"No, I'm fine."

"You can tell me the rest of your story when I get back."

He shuffles down the corridor towards the kitchen, stopping to chat with a tiny old woman who has a curved back like a boomerang. Denis towers over her and has to bend down to talk to her.

When he eventually shuffles back along the corridor, he's clutching two mugs.

"Here, I just made you one," he says, holding a mug out.

"Thanks," I say, taking a sip and then putting it down. It's too hot.

"Milk, no sugar?"

I nod.

"You can't beat a cup of tea," he sighs, though he holds the mug on his lap without drinking from it.

Shafts of sunlight are now hitting the window and it's warm where we sit though I know it will be cold outside. I poked my head out the door this morning but thought better of going for a walk in the garden. It's good to get outside sometimes. Take a stroll across the grass and pretend it's a park, any park, and I'm just another normal person savouring the fresh air.

"Anyone visiting tonight?" Denis asks.

"Don't think so. My mum and dad were up last night."

"What about that pretty girl of yours?"

"Lisa?"

"Is that her name?"

"She won't be coming."

Denis nods. There's something in my voice that tells him not to probe. Lisa's my girlfriend. Was my girlfriend. For six months. Long enough to plan holidays and talk about moving in together but not long enough to stick around when I got sick. She visited once or twice but hated it. She told me it smelt horrible as if she was talking about a filthy toilet or a dirty kitchen.

"That's a shame. Nice-looking girl," Denis mutters.

We drink our tea in comfortable silence. Someone

comes into the room and Denis tells them the TV isn't working before they can turn it on. I know he's lying but I don't say anything.

"So what happened with your hard-on?" he asks, and it sounds so funny when he says it.

"I had it for five days."

"Five days?"

"Swear to God. Five days and it was solid as a rock."

"Every man's dream."

"It was a nightmare."

Denis nods, though I'm sure he's thinking what a new lease of life he'd get if it happened to him.

"So what did you do?" he says. "You've not still got it, have you?"

"No!"

"Thank God for that."

"I went to the doctor on the Wednesday. It was the earliest I could get an appointment. I couldn't go to work. Walking into a classroom would have got me arrested. I tried taping it up but the Sellotape wasn't strong enough. It was terrible. Watching TV, reading, going for a walk, having a shower, lots of showers. But nothing helped."

He shakes his head, taking a sip of tea and frowning. It's gone cold again. Maybe it's just the comfort of having something in his hand? After a couple of minutes I'd gulped mine down. I'm not a big tea drinker but you end up drinking it in here. It helps pass the time.

People bring me books and newspapers and magazines. More than I'll ever be able to read in my lifetime, I always joke, but no-one seems to find it funny. Sometimes I want to read all my favourite books again, just so they're fresh in the memory and other times I try cramming in everything new I can get my hands on, frantically speed-reading and forgetting most of what my eyes have just digested. It won't make any difference anyway. Just another regret to add to the list.

"So what did the doctor say?" Denis asks.

"It was terrible."

"I know. I hate doctors. They've never got good news for you. It's always gloom and doom. 'You've got six months to live, Mr. O'Hara'. Try making that sound upbeat."

"I was sitting in the waiting room flicking through one of those celebrity magazines. Pure rubbish. I was just looking at the pictures of the beautiful women but I couldn't even concentrate on that. I was trying to think what I'd say."

"What did the doctor say?"

"I thought her eyes were going to pop out her head."

"Her? You mean it was a woman doctor?"

I nod.

"Oh, God, that's terrible."

"The worst thing was, she was beautiful. Short brown hair and glasses that made her look really pretty. And just enough lipstick to make me want to kiss her. She took my breath away every time I looked at her. She could have given me a hard-on if I didn't have one already, but I was trying not to look at her because I kept thinking about what was wrong with me, and I didn't know whether I could tell her. I wondered whether to claim I had a sore back but I knew, in my mind, that I couldn't."

I can feel my face heat up as I replay the

conversation that I had with Doctor O'Neill. Catherine.

"It's my penis," I told her.

"Your penis?"

"Yes."

"What's wrong with it?"

"It won't go down."

"Sorry?"

"I've had a hard-on … I mean, erection for five days now."

"Five days?"

"Yes!"

"You've been erect for five days?"

"YES!"

"Five days solid?"

Denis shrieks. "She didn't say that, did she?"

"She did."

He bends over, laughing into his mug of cold tea, shaking so hard some of it spills on to his lap. Someone will think he's wet himself, but that's not unusual in here. Tears are running down his cheeks and he wipes them with his sleeve, sighing as the laughter finally subsides.

I don't want to bore Denis with the details of what happened next. I've told enough of my story for one day. I'm in here so he knows there's no happy ending. It's hardly a proud boast to admit that the man who was permanently hard is now soft all the time.

That's just the way it is in here sometimes. One day you're having a cup of tea with someone, the next there's an empty chair. I sit at the window, staring out at the bulimic trees, but I keep glancing over to where

Denis should be. It happened during the night. I didn't hear a thing. I imagine his family gathered round the bed, the women crying, the men biting quivering lips.

Sandra sneaks up on me and plonks herself down on the other chair. It doesn't seem right. There should be a period of mourning, when the chair is left empty. That's where Denis used to sit, I'll tell anyone who tries to take it and they'll slink off, slightly embarrassed but they'll understand.

"How are you doing?" Sandra asks.

I shrug.

"It's always sad when it happens, isn't it? Even though we should be used to it in here, it doesn't get any easier."

"I know."

Sandra is one of the nurses. She's small and round and cuddly with the biggest pair of breasts I've ever seen. A tremendous feat of engineering, Denis always said. How she manages to stay upright with all that weight trying to pull her down.

"Denis left you this," she says, handing me a carrier bag.

"What is it?"

"I don't know. He just said to give it to you."

"When did he say that?"

"Last night."

"Last night?"

I take the bag and let it rest in my lap.

"It's funny, but sometimes people just know when it's their time," Sandra says. "I've seen it before in here, too many times for it to be a fluke."

"You mean he knew he was going to die?"

"Maybe. I don't know. But he gave this to me last

night and told me it was for you. Said you'd understand."

She stands up and presses her fingers into my shoulder before patting it and walking away. I continue staring at the bag, picturing Denis sipping his tea and staring out the window. I wonder what he thought about when he looked at the trees and the birds and the constant stream of traffic up and down the hill.

I open the bag and look inside. A sheet of notepaper, Denis's shaky handwriting sprawled across the white page.

'Don't let the bastards get you down!!! I'd say think of me when you look at this, but maybe not. Enjoy. Denis.'

I take the magazines out. There are three of them. All glossy. I flick through one of them, glancing at the pictures of naked women, and for the first time in a while, there is the faintest stirring between my legs. I think of Denis and the feeling disappears immediately. I start laughing, loudly, and a couple of people stare as they walk past.

Ordinary World

Neil Connelly sat at the kitchen table, hands cupped round a mug of coffee and looked at each of his three children in turn, giving them what he hoped was a comforting smile. Katie smiled back at him, her toothy grin showing gaps where the last of her baby teeth had recently fallen out. She'd left it under her pillow for the tooth fairy but it was still there the following morning and Neil spent ten minutes convincing her that the fairy would be back that night. She was seven. She accepted whatever he said, but it cost him two pounds.

Luke was ten. He was more interested in dipping chips in a blob of tomato sauce on his plate.

Matthew frowned. "I'm not going," he said.

Neil studied his eldest son, staring into green eyes that were a mirror of Emma's. They never blinked or looked away. Matthew was fifteen. Traces of black hair were dotted along his top lip but too thin to hide the spots which had broken out randomly on his skin. No-one else would notice, though, their eyes focusing instead on the ring which stuck out defiantly at the corner of his mouth.

"You've got an Elvis scowl there," Neil had joked the first time he saw it, though it only made the scowl even more pronounced, especially when Neil had tried a feeble Elvis impersonation.

"You have to come, Matthew."

It was Luke who spoke, through a mouthful of chips.

"What's it got to do with you?" Matthew said.

"Nothing," Luke shrugged. "You just have to go, that's all. Sure he does, dad?"

Neil's eyes darted between his two sons like a tennis spectator. He felt pathetic at having hoped, just for a second, that Luke had come to his rescue, but he was being dragged back into it.

"It's just one day, Matthew. An hour at most."

"No."

"We should all be there. It's important. It's what your mum would have wanted."

He bit his tongue even before the words had carried across the tiny distance between them. Matthew pushed his chair back and stood up. A storm was brewing in his eyes. He started to speak but it tailed off into an angry grunt and he walked out of the kitchen. The front door slammed a few seconds later.

Luke and Katie watched their father, waiting for his own fury, expecting him to chase after their brother and drag him back into the house. Neil looked at them both and tried to muster up another comforting smile but he could tell from their expressions that it hadn't worked.

It was ten o'clock that night before Matthew came home. Neil was watching the news when he heard the door opening. He thought briefly of confronting his son but he wasn't in the mood for a fight. It was best that things were allowed to settle before he brought up the subject again. He'd also apologise for what he said. He still wished he could have rewound the day and started afresh. Why did he have to bring Emma up?

A couple of the stairs creaked as Matthew crept up to his room. Neil just smiled. Tomorrow was another day. He stared at the television though he wasn't concentrating on the sound. There were soldiers and the mangled shell of a car. People were rushing about, some of them drenched in blood like they were extras from a horror film. In the corner of the picture a little girl stood alone, biting her nails.

Through the ceiling a droning noise seeped into the living room and at first he couldn't figure out what it was. He sprung to his feet as soon as he did, bursting out the room and bounding up the stairs two at a time. Katie stood at her bedroom door, eyes barely open as she peered out into the bright hallway. He stopped and scooped her up, carrying her back to bed and dragging the quilt up to her chin.

"It's alright, darling," he whispered, kissing her forehead. "Just go back to sleep."

"It's too noisy," she groaned.

"I know. It'll be okay in a wee minute."

He strode across the hall and pushed open the door with the skull and crossbones poster stuck on it, the word 'DEATH' printed underneath, blood dripping from every letter.

"Turn that thing off," he shouted, searching for the source of the noise. "What the hell are you playing at?" he demanded as Matthew used a remote control to kill the music, the effect only amplifying Neil's voice.

Matthew was sprawled across his bed, back pressed against the headboard, legs crossed. He shrugged.

"They're sleeping. For God's sake, Matthew. Have some sense."

There was a look of insolence on his son's face that was like a burning match to a cannon fuse.

"Do you want me to take that bloody thing out your room?

"Don't care?"

"What is wrong with you these days? You're worse than Luke and Katie."

Neil glanced round the room. The floor was cluttered with DVDs, books, clothes, and dirty plates with bits of half-eaten food; empty crisp packets and plastic bottles of water. He could barely see the carpet. The walls, which he was sure had originally been painted pale green, were completely covered with posters. Marilyn Manson. Nirvana. Slipknot. All watching grotesquely over his son.

Above the headboard he spotted Emma. A tiny smiling face amidst a sea of tortured rebellion. She was laughing. It was a picture he'd taken in Florida at one of the theme parks they'd visited. Superman was giving her a hug and she had a fit of the giggles. Neil's anger drained away like a plug had been pulled out and he was lost for words. He plunged his hands in his pockets and stared at the mess on the floor. Emma used to clean it, nagging Matthew as she did. Now it was his job.

"Matthew, about this morning …"

A defiant frown suddenly appeared on Matthew's face like a gruesome Hallow'een mask.

"I'm sorry. I shouldn't have said anything about your mum."

Matthew nodded. He wasn't going to make it easy. They weren't going to suddenly start crying, or hug and say 'I love you' to each other.

"I'd like you to come with us on Sunday. We all

would. But if you don't want to, then that's up to you."

Neil was sure he spotted the slightest flicker of a smile on Matthew's face but it could have just been that quivering lip playing tricks with his eyes. Whatever it was, it seemed more grateful than resentful and Neil muttered "Goodnight, son," not waiting for a reply as he made his way back downstairs.

Sunday morning was sunny but cold, one of those days which tempt people into wearing flimsier clothes as they look out the window, but which punish them for their folly once they're out of the house.

Katie and Luke were both washed and fed, the pile of dirty clothes and wet towels growing outside the bathroom. Neil could hear the television as he sat in his bedroom. He couldn't tell what was on. That depended on who was in possession of the remote control. If it was Katie, there would be cartoons. Luke always chose the Extreme Sports channel for the skateboarding or mountain-biking or whatever other crazy, limb-breaking activity was on.

Neil hadn't known what to wear. A shirt and tie seemed too formal, jeans and a t-shirt almost disrespectful. He decided on a pair of black trousers with a black zipper and a white polo shirt. He stared at himself in the mirrored wardrobe door which stretched from floor to ceiling. Emma had been dead for a year. A year ago today. Sometimes it felt longer but there were still moments when it seemed like it had just happened. They were going to Mass and then out to visit her. Neil had bought flowers, a giant bouquet of all different kinds. He never could remember her favourite. Katie had made a card, which Luke signed as well, and they were both bringing trowels to tidy up the grave.

Neil shouted down to tell them to put their coats on, then went into the bathroom and splashed cold water over his face. As he walked back out, he nearly bumped into Matthew. He was dressed. Baggy jeans and a black hooded top.

"I'm coming too," he mumbled. Neil nodded. He followed Matthew downstairs and the four of them began the short, weary walk to Mass, retracing their footsteps of a year ago.

Sitting in chapel, Neil was no longer sure if it was such a good idea. It was busy, full of coughs and murmurs, people shuffling in their seats, babies crying, toddlers racing up and down the aisles, throwing tantrums and being dragged to the soundproof crying room at the back. He could hardly concentrate on anything – the priest talking, or remembering Emma. Last time had been different. The sobbing and sniffling of grief was an appropriate soundtrack.

He glanced at his watch, praying it would soon be over. Everyone had sat up, ready to go to Communion. There would only be another ten minutes after that. Neil let Katie and Luke out first to join the queue which stretched up to the priest at the front of the altar. He glanced at Matthew, who sat, head bowed, with his feet on the upturned kneeler. It was enough that he had come to Mass.

A woman was leading the singing, her voice

surging through the microphone and drowning out anyone else who might be joining in. The queue shuffled forward slowly until Neil was standing in front of Father Cassidy. The priest made no acknowledgement of him as he stood, hand thrust out to receive communion. Probably doesn't even remember what day it is, thought Neil, though why would he? He'd have buried many more people since Emma.

As he walked back to his seat, he glanced over at the people still waiting their turn. Matthew was among them. Neil smiled. He noticed heads turning towards his son, imagining the whispers fluttering along the rows.

There's that Connelly boy. Such a shame, losing your mum at that age. He looks so like her as well. Same eyes. It's nice to see him at Mass again.

Neil looked over again at Matthew, who was nearing the priest, and he froze. Matthew had taken off his hooded top. He wore a black t-shirt with the words 'JESUS IS A CUNT' printed in giant white letters on the back. A woman walking behind Neil almost bumped into him and a hold-up quickly emerged as he stared at his son's t-shirt.

There was a gap behind Matthew. The grey-haired man following him was trying to keep his distance. Fingers were pointing, heads shaking, a few voices raised above a whisper. Matthew got to the front and turned away from Father Cassidy without taking communion. He strode to the side and disappeared out the chapel as the priest watched him.

Neil dashed for the back door and ran out into the car park and round to the side of the building but Matthew was gone. He stood, shivering, not sure what to do next. He looked round when he heard crying. Katie and Luke were standing side by side, an older man hovering behind them. They both looked scared. He crouched down and held out his arms. They raced over and he clutched them, whispering words of comfort until Katie stopped crying.

Another hymn was being sung inside. Our God Reigns. They held hands as they walked away.

Lonely In Your Nightmare

S he was old enough to be his mother but she kissed him like she wasn't. He tensed. Surprised. Shocked. But he didn't pull away. They stood toe-to-toe, two shadows boxing in a corner, tongues jostling noisily for dominance. Helen's eyes slowly began to adjust to the dark. Outlines of cuddly toys crept into view. His arms were rigid round her waist. Her hands gripped the back of his neck.

The house was quiet. Empty. Mike was at the pub, laughing and joking with friends and strangers, getting drunker with each passing moment of this lingering kiss. It's what he did now. He would sleep on the couch tonight. Again. That was the unspoken agreement when he was drunk, but it was becoming a comfortable arrangement.

A hand crept slowly over her hip and rested on her bum. Gentle. Apprehensive. She was a teenager again, sitting on a bench in an unlit swing park, fumbling limbs probing to see how far they could get. She smiled.

"What is it?" he asked, breaking off the kiss.

"Nothing."

"What's so funny?"

"It's nothing," she whispered, pulling his head back towards hers. She could feel his resistance.

"Sean, it's nothing."

She locked her lips on to his to silence any further protest and his hands gripped her bum more forcefully. Her fingers forked through his hair. Thick and unruly, it was beneath him to give it any attention. She had often wished for five minutes with a pair of sharp scissors. Now it dawned on her that its untidiness was cultivated, deliberate.

He had appeared one day in their kitchen, standing nervously near the back door as if he was planning to flee at any moment. His eyes were locked on to his feet so it was hard not to notice his hair.

"Mum, this is Sean," said Claire.

"Hi, Sean. Nice to meet you."

His head jerked up briefly as he muttered 'Hi,' and she caught a glimpse of his face. It disappeared from view just as quickly. She smiled at Claire who raised her eyebrows hopefully, searching for parental approval.

Claire had served his name up at dinner one night. Mike didn't notice but that was no surprise. He would float in and out of conversations, contributing little, remembering less. Only when Brendan was home from university would he talk more than he ate as father and son traded football opinions, mother and daughter mute with disinterest.

But Helen heard the name. Sean. Over and over again. She studied her daughter speaking through mouthfuls of spaghetti bolognese. For the first time Helen could see her beauty as a young woman. Seventeen years old, blonde hair resting on her shoulders. They had gone to the hairdressers the week before, just the two of them. Lunch. Shopping. A day to treasure.

It was the sparkle in her eyes that Helen noticed. Those big blue eyes – she got them from her dad – gave her secret away. It was something only a mother would notice and Helen smiled. But it was tinged with sadness. She would always be her baby but she was no longer a child.

Sean's hand slipped under Helen's blouse and his fingers crawled up and down her back. They lingered on her bra strap, then moved away. She felt him press against her leg. He was excited. She began to step back slowly towards the bed. Sean was dragged along like a pin attached to a magnet.

He was in her eye-line. His picture. Stuck on the wall above Claire's desk. Helen knew it was him, even in the dark. She cleaned the room at least twice a week and everything in it was committed to memory; the books scattered on the desk, clothes abandoned over the chair, the framed picture above the bed. And Sean, smiling on the wall. Claire had taken it on holiday, the first time they had gone away together. He was sitting on a rock, the Mediterranean glistening in the background, sunglasses pushed on to the top of his head.

Mike hadn't been happy about it. She had always been his wee girl.

"But she's eighteen," Helen said.

"Well, I think that's too young."

"They've been going out for nearly a year now."

"So?"

"So if they're going to do anything, it doesn't matter if they go away on holiday or not."

He sighed and shook his head as Helen took his hand.

"Trust her, Mike. She's a good girl."

He grunted and she knew he wouldn't protest any

more. Claire had told her first to get her support. Helen tried to remember being eighteen. Her parents would never have agreed even if she'd had the nerve to ask. She could imagine what her father would have said, while her mother silently nodded in the background. The first time she went away with a boy was her honeymoon.

She knew Claire's room so well but misjudged the distance to the bed and they toppled on to it. She lay with Sean on top of her. She tried to slide further up the bed and there was a squeak underneath her.

"What was that?" Sean asked, pushing himself up by his hands. He still hovered over her. Helen laughed.

"Don't worry. It's only this."

She dragged a Minnie Mouse from under her and pressed its tummy. It squeaked. She laughed again and the trace of a smile broke out across Sean's face. Helen threw the toy on to the floor. Sean stared at her. He was serious again. It had been rare to glimpse any other expression but she couldn't really blame him.

Helen didn't waste any time trying to imagine what he was thinking about. He was twenty-two. How could she know what was going through his mind? She could never figure out her own son when he was that age. Brendan would float in and out of their lives like a distant acquaintance. He had been living in Manchester, studying politics and history. He didn't know what he wanted to do now that he was finished but he didn't seem to care. Any time they tried to ask him, he'd just shrug and mumble vaguely.

Mike would sometimes lose patience but Helen tried not to join in the criticism. There was a girl, Frankie, who had followed him back to Glasgow. Helen would sometimes meet her for lunch. Helen liked her. She was confident, determined, organised. She knew Frankie was good for her son. And she was good for Helen as well.

They started kissing again but Helen wasn't comfortable. Sean's hip was pressing against her and though she tried moving under him, it made no difference.

"Let me up," she said.

"What's wrong?"

"Nothing."

He rolled off her and stood at the edge of the bed. She guided him back and he sat down as she stood in front of him. She began unbuttoning her blouse as he watched, hands clasped together in his lap as if in prayer. Helen's fingers were trembling. Her blouse hung open and they stared at each other, neither wanting to blink or look away. She let the blouse fall silently to the floor, then unclipped her bra and slipped it off.

She shivered. She didn't know what to do with her arms. Should she fold them? Let them hang awkwardly at her side? Put her hands on her hips? Defiant. She had been in control right up to this moment. Now she felt nervous.

He was staring at her. At her breasts. She wanted to know what he was thinking. Of her. Of them. Would he compare them to Claire's? But that wasn't fair. Helen was older. Forty-nine. With two kids.

What did her expect? If he had seen her twenty-five years ago, before Brendan, before Claire, he would have seen her as she was meant to be.

Sean stretched out his hand and touched hers, tugging her towards him. Their knees collided and his lips kissed her nipple. Gently. She closed her eyes and ran her fingers through his hair. The minutes drifted by as he continued kissing her breasts. It felt strange. Helen couldn't remember the last time anyone other than Mike had touched her. She felt relaxed, almost sleepy. Sean's tongue teased and traced as his hands tugged at the zip of her skirt. There was only silence in the room. She could barely hear him breathe.

He would have sat here before in this room, with Claire standing where Helen was now. Maybe she was on his mind now. Claire. His fiancée.

They had sat like giggling teenagers – they were twenty-one – as Claire broke the news. Helen hugged her daughter while the two men shook hands, a nod from the elder to the younger. A bottle of wine appeared and laughter filled the house. They were talking about their future but no date had been set.

"We're still young," Claire said. "We'll probably wait four or five years."

Helen wanted to ask why. Why now? What was the point? Making plans but planning nothing. Her own engagement had only been six months. But she knew what the answer would be, and she couldn't argue with 'love' even if she wanted to.

Yet wedding brochures did appear, and the house echoed with talk of dresses and cakes and photographers and reception venues and cars and bridesmaids. Mother and daughter would whisper conspiratorially while Mike contributed occasional references to the cost of it all. Claire just laughed and told him she and Sean were saving up. He wasn't convinced.

Sean was on top of her. His head buried into her neck as he thrust silently back and forth. Helen gripped his back, like a cat with a claw-cushion. Her eyes were shut. Tight. She tried to forget where she was, who she was. She wanted to be someone else, but it was impossible. Not now. Not here.

Claire's bed. Where she had slept since she outgrew her cot. Well, maybe not the same one. They had changed it once or twice. Claire kept appearing behind her eyes, sometimes a child, sometimes a woman. Always her daughter. Helen wasn't religious but she wondered if her daughter was watching her. What would she be thinking? What could Helen say? There were no words. She dug her nails deeper into Sean's skin. He flinched. Her legs were wrapped around his and she could feel his hot skin against her own. Still, she shivered.

It wasn't the first time she had imagined Claire watching her. Sometimes she would talk to her when she was on her own, usually in this room. She would tell her what was going on.

'Your dad's still at West Park. They wanted him to go for the assistant head's job but he didn't fancy it. Said he'd miss the classroom too much. You know what he's like. And your brother's doing well. You know he moved back up to Glasgow? He wanted to be closer to home. He's got a job on a newspaper.

Frankie moved up too. I think you met her once. She's nice. You'd like her. And me? I'm doing okay, darling. Don't you worry about me. I'll be fine.'

They lay together in silence, his head resting on her chest. She could feel his breath on her breasts, his heartbeat on her stomach, the hairs on his legs brushing against her smooth limbs. Would they have done this? Sean and her daughter. Claire. Her beautiful baby.

He sprung up almost as soon as his first tear caressed her skin. Helen had only seen him cry once. At Claire's funeral. Out the corner of her watery eye. He wept into his hands while his mum threw a helpless arm around his shoulders.

Helen rolled herself in the duvet and faced the wall as Sean dressed quickly. The door creaked as he made his escape. She was glad to be on her own now, relieved that there had been no awkward words. What could they have talked about with so many years between them? The one thing that linked them was the only thing they could never mention.

Now she could hear voices. Deep. Loud. Mike was home. Pouring another drink. Trying to persuade Sean to join him.

She buried her head into the pillow and took a deep breath. She wanted it to remind her of Claire, like freshly peeled apples that used to follow her from room to room even after Claire had moved out. But she could only smell him. Sean. And that felt right as well in this room. She had washed him out of these covers so many times before.

Mike was talking loudly, no doubt standing in

front of the TV, glass in hand, taking gulps between every sentence while Sean nursed his own drink. Being reminded every few minutes to 'Get it down you.' There would probably be two men falling asleep on the couch tonight.

A View To A Kill

I wasn't sure that going to the school reunion was a good idea. In fact, I knew it was a bad idea, but Stevie was persistent and persuasive.

"It'll be a laugh," he said.

"I don't think it will be."

"Do you not want to see how everyone turned out?"

"No."

"Well, what about the girls?"

"What about them?"

"Are you not curious to find out if the ones you thought were good-looking at school are still the best-looking ones now."

"It's thirty years ago."

"So?"

"So look at us... Okay, look at me. Look what thirty years has done to me."

"That's a fair point... But I still think it'll be a laugh. You'll regret it if you don't go."

"I won't."

There was a warning voice whispering urgently inside my head, offering contradictory advice to the counsel from my friend, but it wasn't loud enough. Stevie wanted to go. Why wouldn't he? He was the most famous person ever to have gone to St Angela's Secondary School, the most famous person to come out of the town of West Park even. People would be coming to the reunion just to see him, to talk to him, to get their picture taken with him, even just to say they'd been in the same room as the lead singer of The Edible Bricks; I was sure there would be faces I wouldn't recognise because they hadn't actually been at school with us. Fame was a powerful magnet, drawing in admirers from near and far. It was pulling me too, reluctantly, towards the school reunion, even if it was the last place I wanted to be.

People would probably think I was a minder, brought along to ensure that a respectful distance was kept between them and Stevie, not realising that I'd once sat in the same classroom as them. I looked at myself in the full-length mirrored wardrobe door and could understand why they'd make that mistake. Sometimes I didn't even recognise myself. My hair was gone – the portents had been there back in school with the hairline creeping up my forehead like the tide going out – revealing a bumpy and scarred skull. Grey stubble covered my weary face while lines spread out from the corners of my eyes like B-roads on a map.

I dropped the towel that was wrapped round my waist and studied my naked body. When I turned and stood side-on, my hands stroked my belly like I was the world's first, and hairiest pregnant man, ready to give birth at any moment. Even when I breathed in, it still looked like I was expecting, though only about four or five months gone. I couldn't bend over and touch my toes, and I couldn't remember the last time I could look down and see my dick without having to strain my neck. I picked the towel up and threw it on the bed before putting a pair of boxer shorts on.

Thirty years was a long time, I knew, and it was impossible to resist the ravages of time – well, unless you were a rich and successful pop star – but I feared that when the Class of '83 lined up for the inevitable group picture at some point during the evening, the camera would reveal that those years had been crueller to me than most.

It wasn't that I had anyone else to blame. It was my own fault, though accepting this fact didn't make me feel any better or any more enthusiastic about rekindling contact with people I'd once spent most of my waking hours with, but who had been strangers to me for three decades now. If only I had formed a band when I left St Angela's, had written some of the most anthemic tunes of the 1980s, sold enough records to make me as rich as Croesus – I remembered at least one thing from first-year Latin classes – and then spent the following years travelling the world and basking in the adulation that seemed to glow like an eternal sunset. The biggest surprise was that Stevie and I had remained friends even as our lives took vastly different trajectories.

I didn't know why that was, and it wasn't something we discussed or analysed, at least not when we met up. I thought about it a lot, though, when I was sitting in my flat or driving a group of drunks home that I'd picked up after a night out, trying to ignore the shouting and swearing and takeaway food that always threatened to spill on to the seats, or the sudden explosions of vomit that would fill the taxi with an odour I couldn't scrub away for days; I knew Stevie was probably lying in the French sunshine, sipping cocktails or straddling the latest model girlfriend he had acquired. I never uncovered the answer, however, and I didn't think I ever would. Maybe there was no answer. We were just friends, and that was enough, sharing a history that stretched back into the distant past and a time before Stevie was famous and I was still thin. We swapped text messages, sent emails, enjoyed phone-calls debating football, politics, religion and the relative merits of *Field of Dreams*; we never spoke about music.

St Angela's sat on the edge of West Park, hanging precariously on to the town's boundary so that it didn't drop into Glasgow. There were middle-class sensibilities and snobbery to appease, after all. We decided to walk to the school, even though a taxi would have been my preferred mode of transport; Stevie would have arrived in a limousine. Maybe I was being unfair. It was his suggestion that we meet up in the centre of the town and then retrace the footsteps of our own past. It was actually a good idea.

"Unless it's pouring," Stevie said. "Then we'll take the limo."

He was leaning against a lamppost outside a Costa Coffee shop, a recent addition to West Park's façade, as I approached. It had previously been a jeweller's and before that... It was stretching my memory to conjure up images of the row of shops which had changed shape and identity so many times since 1983. I knew Stevie thought he was being inconspicuous, just another denizen of the town waiting for the next bus or the arrival of his wife from a shopping exhibition in the nearby supermarket. The shades gave him away, though, a needless piece of attire on a cold and cloudy September evening. That, and the green, skin-tight jeans, silver training shoes that looked as though they'd been stolen from the set of

Back To The Future, and a black dinner jacket with the collar turned up. For a fleeting moment, I thought of turning and walking away, heading for the refuge of Devlin's, the local pub that had first welcomed us as nervous seventeen-year-old drinking virgins.

As I hesitated, Stevie spotted me and pushed himself off the lamppost, waving as he did so. I waved back without much enthusiasm, and trudged forward, though Stevie's journey was halted when a woman and her husband stopped him and asked for a picture, the hapless husband forced into the role of photographer while his wife cuddled into Stevie. Did he not realise that she'd be dreaming of Stevie next time they had sex? I hovered on the periphery until Stevie had managed to extricate himself and then we began walking.

"Remember the time we took up stealing for Lent?" he asked as we passed where the John Menzies shop used to be. We'd plundered its shelves every morning on the way to school.

"My mum would have killed me if we'd have been caught."

"It did make a change from giving up sweets or chocolate, though."

There was a familiarity to the journey, each step unlocking another section of the picture that was forever imbedded in my mind, though long since forgotten. It was like an episode of *Catchphrase*, and I'd eventually shout out the answer when I realised what it was. Many of the houses had changed. It had been thirty years since we'd trodden this path, so that was hardly surprising, but some things still looked the same; a window frame or a tree in the middle of the garden beginning to shed its pink petals all over the grass. There were different cars now, and more of them. Yet I knew instinctively where I was going – we both did – and if we'd closed our eyes, I was sure we would still be able to find our way to St Angela's.

Neither of us spoke much, and what snatches of conversation there had been dried up as we got closer to the school. I stopped at the corner of Eastfield Avenue, and Stevie did too, a few steps further forward.

"Are you okay?" he said.

"I think so."

"Don't bottle out of it now, Paul."

"We could just head to the pub."

"Come on, man. We're nearly there. The pub's miles away."

"This is going to be shite."

"It'll be fine... Listen, if it is shite, then we can go."

"I don't know why you're so keen to be there."

"I just think it'll be a laugh."

He started to walk away, heading towards the corner where I knew the edifice of our old school would loom large before us.

"And I'm going to pump Bernie Doherty."

"What the fuck?"

He disappeared round the corner as I broke into a jog to catch up with him, the name 'Bernie Doherty' rattling round my head like a thirty-year-old echo.

If I had an illustrated dictionary, then Bernie Doherty's 17-year-old face would be there when I looked up the phrase 'unrequited love'; if I actually owned a dictionary with pictures, then I'd be going to the reunion with a dunce's cap on.

I loved Bernie Doherty with a passion that was physically painful, and it was a pain that I suffered in silence from the summer of 1982 right through until the day I left St Angela's, and beyond too. We had met one day in a park just behind the main road of the town, an accidental encounter that I sometimes later wished had never happened. We had never really spoken although we'd spent the previous four years at the same school, even sharing the same classroom on occasion. I said hello, expecting no more in return, but she stopped, and so I did too. Nearly an hour later, after we talked about everything and nothing – music and TV programmes, exam results and people at school – I went my way and she went hers. By the time I got home, I felt sick and light-headed and confused and giddy and euphoric and depressed all in one. I didn't know it then but I was in love.

Not that I did anything about my new status, except pine in the solitary confinement of my bedroom, listening to Joy Division albums over and over again. Not even Stevie knew how I felt. I couldn't tell him. I didn't know how to, and even if he'd be sympathetic when I poured out my heart, I knew that I'd be mercilessly teased at school when everyone found out; those were just the rules of the playground. I accepted and abided by them myself, and so I couldn't have complained if I ended up the victim. So I said nothing, and hoped that the longing gazes I threw in Bernie's direction remained discreet enough that no-one other than her would notice. They turned out to be so discreet that even she remained oblivious.

Now I was going to see her again, for the first time since the 1980s, and I knew I'd remain just as tongue-tied, forced to stand as a silent witness while the legendary Stevie Gallagher, lead singer of Scotland's most successful band after Simple Minds, moved in with his silver tongue and golden voice and platinum albums and swept her off her feet. My only hope was that Bernie wouldn't be there.

The school had changed since we had walked out through its gates for the last time, in June 1983, not looking back in anger or regret, or even with fondness for a place that, if I was being honest, I had actually enjoyed being part of. It wasn't that the intervening thirty years had taken its inevitable toll on the school building in much the same way that time had done with me. It was actually a new building.

The old school, the one that we remembered, was gone, reduced to rubble about five years ago and with it, our memories; names etched with a compass on the wooden desks, dents in walls where clowning about escalated into full-scale fights, footprints and voices that had floated through the corridors down the years. The new building wasn't unwelcoming but it was unfamiliar. The reunion could have been held anywhere, for all that it was being held on the same site.

A giant poster greeted us as we stepped through the front door, along with a ripple of whispers as people spotted Stevie. The poster had four photographs making up the full image, pictures of the four 'house' groups which made up the year – Ogilvie, Sinclair, Kentigern and Marian. I was in the Ogilvie picture. Above it was printed the words 'WELCOME TO THE CLASS OF '83'.

I hung back as bodies were drawn inexorably towards Stevie. He glanced over his shoulder and shrugged, helplessly, but I knew that he enjoyed the handshakes and backslaps and photographs and autographs. It was strange to think that former school friends has become fans, enthusiastically greeted but instantly forgotten. It didn't seem to bother them, or the teachers too, most of whom, I realised, were far too young to have been at school when we were here.

At least there was alcohol on sale and we didn't have to hide our carry-outs round the back of the school and sneak them in through a classroom window while someone kept watch at the door. The bar was set up in the area normally used to cook the school dinners and a queue had already formed. I took my place at the end and kept my gaze on the empty hall which the organisers hoped would soon fill up with middle-aged dancers. No doubt alcohol would coax them on to the floor if the medley of music from our teenage years didn't provoke the same reaction. Billy Ocean was reverberating round the hall, which seemed cavernous, as groups gathered at the side. *When The Going Gets Tough, The Tough Get Going.*

I thought I recognised a few faces – mainly female ones – and it seemed as though people were gravitating towards the same group of friends they'd had all those years ago. My eyes searched for my own friends, nicknames immediately springing to mind that I'm sure had been shed when everyone stepped into the adult world. Douldy, Bronzo, Falzo, Shug, Rubiks. Stevie was always Gallo while I was Maguire. Nothing funny or fancy. Just my surname.

There were three guys standing at the other end of

the bar talking, and one of them looked like Rubiks, or more like Rubiks' dad now. His real name was Tony Devlin, and he'd hated his nickname at school. He'd only got it on account of having been able to complete the Rubik's Cube in under a minute. Forty-two seconds was his best time. No-one else in the school had come anywhere close to that. At first he hadn't minded. He was a minor celebrity in Saint Angela's for about ten minutes but that novelty had soon worn off when everyone got bored of the Rubik's Cube, and Tony quickly grew tired of the nickname too. It hadn't stopped the rest of us calling him it, particularly when we saw that it annoyed him, though it was always a judgement call. Tony had a temper and, if pushed, was ready for a square-go with whoever riled him.

I knew that Shug wouldn't be here. My mum had seen the notice in the *Evening Times* a couple of years ago and phoned to tell me. 'Peacefully after a short illness,' the announcement said. He'd been married with a couple of kids. I hadn't seen him since we left school, and I didn't know where he had lived or what he did. It was still sad, though. I wondered who else from the class of '83 wouldn't have lasted the distance.

I didn't really want to talk to my former friends – if that's who they were – at least not until I'd had a few drinks, and so I took my bottle of beer and drifted off in the opposite direction, content to stand on my own, though I realised I'd quickly have to return to the bar since, with two gulps, the bottle was almost empty. I started back towards the bar and collided with someone.

"Sorry," I mumbled.

"Paul?"

"Yes."

"Paul Maguire?"

"Yes."

I took a step back and looked her up and down. It was Bernie Doherty.

I was sixteen again, standing closer to Bernie that I had ever been before unless we found ourselves accidentally sitting side by side in the classroom, yet the distance of thirty years between then and now hadn't made me any more articulate, and so I stared in silence.

"Are you okay? Paul? Paul?"

"Sorry, I was miles away."

"Nineteen eighty-three?"

"Yes," I said.

"It's weird, isn't it, being back here again after all these years."

"And it's not even the same school, well, the same building."

"I know. I wasn't even sure about coming."

"Me neither."

I wanted her to tell me she was glad that I was here, and that she'd had a massive crush on me when we were at school but was too shy to say anything, and it was something that she'd regretted for the past thirty years, always wondering how her life might have turned out if only she had. Then I remembered that was me who felt all those things.

A sudden countdown being shouted from one of the tables lining either side of the hall caused us both to look round. Glasses were slammed on the table and then thrown down throats before a chorus of squeals and shouts took over.

"Jäger bombs," Bernie said.

"Who is that?"

"Carolyn Quinn, Elaine McDermott and Pauline Nolan. I don't know who the other two are."

"I thought you and Carolyn were friends."

"We were, a long time ago. A lot's happened since then. I mean, it's not like you and Stevie Gallagher are still in touch."

As if on cue, a commotion erupted at the far end of the hall as Stevie walked in, already accompanied by a coterie of admirers, male and female.

"Talk of the devil," said Bernie. "Look at the state of him … Act your age, you tosser!" she shouted, though her words were lost in the maelstrom of noise swirling round the room. Blancmange were singing *Living On the Ceiling*, and another round of jäger bombs were being counted down.

Stevie spotted me and waved, though to the untrained eye, it could have been towards anyone. A few hands were raised automatically, trying to claim the recognition for their own.

"Oh God, he's heading this way," said Bernie. "Do you think he'll be offended if I tell him I think his music's shite?"

"I'm sure you won't be the first person to tell him that, or the last."

Stevie had managed to shrug off most of the hangers-on, a skill he'd honed through many years of practice, and now strode towards us.

"I could murder a beer, man," he said when he reached us.

"No worries, I've nearly finished this one."

I could sense Bernie staring at me.

"Hi," Stevie said, holding out his hand. "Stevie Gallagher."

"Yes, I know who you are," Bernie said, shaking it briefly.

"And you are?"

"This is Bernie Doherty," I said.

"I know that. I recognised you right away. How are you doing, Bernie?"

"I'm good."

"It's great to see you. You look fantastic."

"Do you want a drink, Bernie?" I asked.

"Sure. Vodka and diet coke, please."

I stood at the bar, even after getting served, and watched Stevie at work, leaning in close, whispering in her ear, getting her to laugh, draping his arm across her shoulder and leaving it there for just a few seconds too long. I wondered where they'd end up, maybe in the changing rooms in the PE block or one of the chemistry labs. Maybe he'd whisk her off to some fancy hotel in Glasgow.

I gulped down Bernie's vodka and then waited to order another one. When I got back with the drinks, Bernie was on the point of leaving.

"Thanks, Paul," she said, talking the plastic glass from me. "That's one I owe you. I've just spotted Frances Welsh, so I'm just going to go and say hello. Maybe see you later?"

"Sure," I said.

"Nice seeing you again, Bernie," Stevie said, wrapping her in a hug. "Catch you later."

She managed to shrug him off and walked away.

"I'm in there, old boy," Stevie said, licking his lips and then moving the bottle of beer in and out of his mouth as he grinned. For that split second I hated him and his skinny jeans and his sunglasses and his dyed black hair.

There was a lot of drinking going on, perhaps making up for the fact we were forbidden to do so when we were pupils. I was on my sixth bottle of beer and an hour had not yet past since we'd arrived. Clusters of people gathered outside to smoke, sending tiny clouds into the air; you could smell them before you saw them when they returned inside.

Stevie had once again been swept away by a wave of adulation, though I would occasionally see his head bobbing up and down in the middle of the sea of bodies which threatened to submerge him. People were filling up the dance floor, mainly the women, but a few of the guys were up as well. I watched them with a mixture of pity and scorn; men over the age of thirty should not dance in public, because they can't.

I had exchanged words with a few people. Working? Yes. Married? No. Children? Yes, a daughter. What's her name? Ariel. Her mother was a *Little Mermaid* fan, I explained with a helpless shrug. It might have been few words with a lot of people. Already, I couldn't remember. I was content to stand on my own, hoping to catch a glimpse of Bernie as she moved from table to table; she had always been one of the most popular people in school. She was at the jäger bombs' table now, smiling and nodding as more alcohol was thrown down already lubricated necks; she declined all offers of a glass.

A cheer went up that rippled across the hall until it reached the tables at the back. Stevie was on stage alongside Mr Murdoch, the headteacher, who stood in front of a microphone. Stevie was behind him, a guitar slung over his shoulder. He was busy tuning it but looked up and out into the crowd every few seconds, flashing a grin for each eager face staring back at him.

"I'm delighted to have you, the Class of 1983, back here at St Angela's tonight," Mr Murdoch said. "And I hope this event will bring back some very happy memories of the time you spent at the school."

"Hurry up and get on with it, baldy!" It was Pauline Nolan.

Her friends started laughing but Bernie just stared. If Mr Murdoch had heard her, he didn't give any indication, but kept on talking.

"We're also delighted to have one of our most famous former pupils with us tonight. I'm sure you all remember Stevie Gallagher."

More cheers, mainly female voices.

"And I'm very excited to tell you that Stevie has kindly agreed to perform a couple of his songs for us tonight."

Louder cheers, again mainly from the women in the hall. I saw a smile break out across Stevie's face and realised that's why he had wanted to come. He was rich, he was famous, but now he was being adored by everyone who knew him before all of that. He wasn't a former classmate, a peer, a friend; he was an idol, up on stage and looking down on everyone else. Maybe it was the thrill of the cheers he was addicted to.

Mr Murdoch moved away and Stevie stepped up to the microphone, waiting for about thirty seconds to mop up every last drop of applause.

"Hello, St Angela's!"

Cheers.

"It's great to be back, isn't it?"

More cheers.

"I'm going to play you a little song now … You might have heard it before."

He took a step back and began playing the opening riff of *Venetian Banana*, his most famous song. The cheers got even louder and many people were gravitating towards the stage. It was a great song – shite title, though – but it had helped make The Edible Bricks, and Stevie, rich and famous beyond his wildest dreams. The jäger bomb table were all on their feet, though Bernie remained sitting. She looked round and caught my eye, shaking her head and rolling her eyes. I smiled.

Stevie's voice filled the hall and the lights from mobile phones held above heads to record the moment for posterity – or Facebook, more likely – offered an atmospheric illumination; in 1983 we'd have been holding cigarette lighters. There was no denying he had a great voice. It was strange whenever he came on the radio; I'd be out in the taxi, perhaps waiting at the rank, and then he'd be singing to me, his friend, and I'd always look round, hoping to find someone I could tell that I knew the voice on the radio, but there never seemed to be anyone there.

As Stevie got to the end of the song, he was drowned out by a tumult of cheers and I could see that it was like oxygen for him. I joined in the applause too. Why not? He deserved it, and he was my friend.

"I'd like to play a song now that will take us all back to 1983," Stevie was saying into the microphone, slightly breathless. "It was one of the first songs which made me want to be in a band, and it still sounds as good today as it did all those years ago ... I hope you like it."

He started playing the guitar though I didn't immediately recognise the tune. It was only when he started singing that I realised it was *Rio*.

"Duran Duran are shite!"

I looked round at the jäger bomb table. Carolyn Quinn was on her feet, trying to clamber up on to the seat, though her tight skirt was preventing her from lifting her foot up.

"Give us some Spandau Ballet," she shouted and the rest of the table cheered. Everyone except Bernie.

"Shut the fuck up, Carolyn," Bernie said.

I edged closer to the table.

"What did you say?" Carolyn asked.

"I said, shut the fuck up. Are you deaf as well as drunk?"

"Who do you think you're talking to?"

Bernie shook her head and turned away, staring towards the stage.

"Duran Duran cow," Carolyn said.

"Spandau Ballet bitch," said Bernie, standing up.

I was on the periphery of the table now, but still too far away to stop Carolyn launching herself towards Bernie, though she banged into the edge of the table as she did so, which deflected the force of her attack. She pushed Bernie, who stumbled back a couple of steps, knocking her chair over, though she quickly recovered and sprung forward, throwing a punch which hit Carolyn in the mouth, knocking her to the floor. Then Bernie was on top of her as screams threatened to drown out Stevie's song. She was slapping Carolyn, pulling her hair and trying to rip her blouse off as Carolyn shielded her face while, at the same time, attempted to kick Bernie's back.

Some of the jäger bomb table, temporarily stunned by the sudden attack, came to their friend's aid and Bernie was bundled off Carolyn. She rolled on to the floor and I stepped in just as Pauline Nolan swung a leg as her. I pushed Pauline out the way, watching her topple to the ground, and helped Bernie to her feet.

Leave me alone," she shouted, giving me a firm push and then striding off in the opposite direction, through a set of doors and into the darkness of the school corridors that were, to all intents and purposes, out of bounds.

I finished my beer and put the empty bottle down on the table beside the collection I'd managed to assemble. Bernie hadn't returned even though the fight had been over for half an hour at least. Stevie had disappeared too, vanishing into the labyrinth of the new school once I told him what had happened. I knew he wanted to play the knight in shining armour.

I tried to blot out what I knew was going on, hoping to drown the images in alcohol, but it didn't work. There wasn't enough beer in the school. I even tried speaking to some people, but either they were really boring, or I was. Either way, the conversations were short, painful and instantly forgettable. I knew I should leave, and hope that when I woke up in the morning, I'd discover it had all just been a horrible dream. Instead, I pushed open the doors and stepped into the darkness too.

I found myself walking on tip-toe along the

corridor, not wanting to alert anyone to my approach. I heard a low groan from the classroom up ahead on my left and I stopped, holding my breath for a few seconds before moving forward again with even greater stealth than before.

I pushed open the classroom door and peered into the darkness.

"Bernie?" I whispered.

Out of the gloom I could make out a figure leaning against the teacher's desk. There was another figure kneeling on the floor in front of them, head bobbing back and forth, a ghostly figure in a white blouse. Stevie glanced up and spotted me. He grinned, giving me a thumbs-up sign with his right hand while his left hand continued gripping the brown hair of the kneeling figure. Bernie.

I shook my head and closed the door, standing outside with my forehead leaning against the glass panel, letting its cool surface soothe me. I wasn't going to wait for Stevie. I couldn't. I'd ignore his calls too, and the text messages. He'd want to tell me all about it, and with relish, but the thought of hearing all the graphic details was too much to bear.

"Are you okay? Paul? Paul?"

I looked round.

"Bernie?"

"Are you alright?"

"I don't know."

"You look like you've seen a ghost."

I stared through the glass again and then back at Bernie.

"I think I did."

"I'm heading off now so I just wanted to say goodbye."

"Okay."

I glanced over my shoulder quickly into the classroom, but I couldn't see anything in the gloom.

"Where were you?" I asked.

"I was just in the staffroom upstairs, hiding there until I calmed down."

"What was that all about?"

"It's a long story."

"You can tell me … if you want to cut a long story short?"

"Ha, ha. Very funny," she said, gently pushing my arm.

I looked back again at the classroom, and smiled.

"Are you sure you're okay?" she said.

"Yes, I'm fine."

"It was nice to see you again."

"You too."

We stood facing each other for a few moments.

"So … Bye then," Bernie said.

"Bye."

She turned to walk away.

"Bernie."

"Yes?"

"Do you fancy going for a drink?"

"Well, it's late and I've got work in the morning and…"

"No problem, it's fine."

"No, I'm not saying no. Just not now. Next week maybe?"

"Next week?"

"If you're not busy."

"I'm not busy."

"A drink would be nice then," she said.

"Good … Good."

We started walking down the corridor, heading towards the music, which was getting louder. Depeche Mode's *Just Can't Get Enough*. It was as easy as that. All I had to do was ask. If only I had known that thirty years ago. If only I could back and whisper some words of wisdom to my teenage self, and tell him to put away the poetry and toilet roll and just ask a girl out. The worst thing that could happen would be that she said no. But she might say yes. She said yes.

"Oh God, what does she want now?"

Carolyn Quinn was walking towards us with a purpose that visibly dissipated when she realised who was ahead of her. When she halted, she was still a couple of feet from us, just outside of Bernie's range. Her lip was already swollen and her blonde hair had still not managed to regain its previous perfection; there was a rip on the shoulder of her blouse.

"Have you seen Allan?" she said, nervously.

"Allan?"

"My husband. I can't find him anywhere. He's supposed to be running us all home."

"Sorry, I haven't seen him," Bernie said.

"Was he wearing a white shirt?" I asked.

"What?"

"Did he have a white shirt on?"

"I think so. Yes."

"Brown hair?"

She nodded. I glanced over my shoulder back along the corridor.

"Try that classroom," I said, pointing towards the door. "I'm sure I saw someone in there."

"Thanks," she muttered, walking past us warily, keeping me as a barrier between her and Bernie.

"Come on, let's get out of here," Bernie said, taking my hand and leading the way. It felt nice and I told myself I was never going to let go.

Pressure Off

The slice of banoffee pie sat on its own in the glass cabinet, a lonely presence on otherwise empty shelves, like the fat kid at a game of playground football, left standing against the wall while the two team captains fought over him; the loser was the one who had to include him in his team. If I ignored it now, it would probably end up in the bin, gone, forgotten and never to fulfil its destiny as a cake to be eaten and enjoyed. Jesus, I was tired. It had been a long shift. I rubbed my eyes and shook my head, hoping to dispel the nonsense swirling inside my head. More than tired, however, I was hungry. A slice of pie and a cup of black coffee would provide welcome sustenance until I got home.

I glanced around the café. A grey-haired man was sitting in the far corner, staring into his cup like he was trying to divine what the tea leaves meant. Across from him two girls were putting their coats on while maintaining a conversation and trying to text at the same time. A woman wearing a burgundy overall on top of a black t-shirt and matching skirt was leaning across one of the tables wiping it clean. I stared at her, although I kept glancing at the other people in the café in case anyone had clocked me; I didn't want them to think I was leering at her. Maybe I was, but my defence was that I was trying to catch her attention. I should have called to her, or coughed too loudly so that she turned round, but I just kept staring at her legs.

She stood up, stretching slowly and carefully, and

then looked back towards the counter. I smiled hopefully. She put down the cloth on the table, wiping her hands on her overall and then walked towards me.

"We're closed," she said.

I looked over at the grey-haired man and then back at her.

"It was just a quick cup of coffee I was after."

She walked passed me and leaned in through a door behind the counter and brought out a mop and bucket.

"I've already cashed up," she said, nodding at the till.

"I was going to take that banoffee pie as well. It'll save you having to throw it out."

She glanced over at the cake shelves, the hint of a smile twitching at the edge of her mouth, and then back at me. The café door opened and we both looked round as the two girls walked out into the night.

"It's just the dregs of the coffee pot," she said. "Everything's switched off."

"That's fine by me."

She rested the mop against the counter and picked up the pot, pouring the black liquid into a cardboard cup normally used for takeaway customers. She handed it to me and then brought out the solitary slice of pie. I put the cup down on the counter beside the plate and pulled some change out of my pocket.

"It's on the house," she said.

"Are you sure?"

"As long as you're quick."

I sat down at the table nearest the counter and took a gulp of coffee. It was only vaguely warm but I made sure to nod and smile. She picked up the bucket with one hand, holding on to the mop with the other, and walked over to the far side of the café. I watched her washing down the floor as I ate the banoffee pie. It was delicious, the caramel filling with cream and bananas smooth on my tongue. I crunched through the base. I knew she couldn't hear me eating but it sounded loud in the emptiness.

The grey-haired man was on his feet now, slipping into his long coat like it was an extra layer of skin. He picked up a book that was lying on the table and then walked towards the door, making an exaggerated detour away from where the floor was already wet.

"Goodnight," the woman said, leaning on her mop, receiving a slight bow in reply.

She looked over at me when the door closed behind the man and I took another piece of the pie, holding my free hand under my chin to catch any stray crumbs. It reminded me of being an altar boy, standing beside the priest as he doled out communion while I held a small gold plate at chest-height to each person, ready to catch the holy wafer if it should spill out of their mouth for any reason. I was leaving the coffee to the end – the bitter end – when I'd drain the cup in one gulp and hope it didn't spoil the taste of the pie which lingered in my mouth.

"Busy day?" I asked as she stopped mopping the floor and stretched again, holding her back and wincing.

"A long day."

"What time did you start?"

"Twelve o'clock."

"That is a long day."

"Tell me about it. I'm absolutely shattered. I just

want to finish here, get up the road and put my feet up."

"Sorry. I'm keeping you back." I pushed another piece of pie into my mouth.

"No, you're fine. I'll be another five minutes anyway."

She resumed mopping the floor. I glanced at the clock on the wall behind the counter, watching the second hand spin round the face in a never-ending race with itself. It was just after ten. It had been a long day for me too. My shift started at eight this morning and had stretched into forever, lifting and carrying and fetching and delivering, all the while casting envious glances at the smokers huddled together under the shelter erected at the back of the warehouse which provided little protection against the elements. At least they got intermittent breaks without having to wait for the lunch-hour which felt like an eternity in arriving but seemed to be over in the blink of an eye. I knew I should never have quit smoking.

I finished the pie and dropped the small fork noisily on to the plate. The woman looked up.

"That was magic," I said. "Thanks."

She propped the mop against a table and walked over to me, picking up the plate.

"Good. I'm glad you enjoyed it."

She smiled, a proper smile that, just for a second, managed to push away the tired lines which stretched out from the edges of her eyes. I didn't want to stare at her, but her blue eyes were hard to ignore. Her face was pale and wore no trace of make-up while there was a cold sore above her top lip at the right-hand corner of her mouth. Whenever I looked at her, she would touch it, conscious of it while trying to conceal it at the same time. Her hair was brown and blonde and grey, and pulled back into a tight ponytail which dangled at her shoulder. A silver chain peeked out above the collar of her t-shirt, resting on a thin neck. Her hands were wrinkled and worn, a solitary gold ring the only jewellery on her fingers, although she also had a watch round her left wrist.

"With these hands I give you my heart, crowned with love."

"What?"

"Your ring… Sorry, it's just that I saw it was a Claddagh ring."

"This?" She held her right hand up to her face like she hadn't realised she was wearing the ring and was now studying it for the first time.

"It was my mum's," she said.

"My mum wore one too."

"Did she?"

"It was her wedding ring."

"Have you still got it?"

"No. My sister might have it but I don't know. I've never asked her."

She played with the ring nervously, moving it along her finger or twisting it. The heart was pointing outwards, looking for love or perhaps just waiting, more in hope than expectation. Maybe the hope had gone but she wasn't going to turn it inwards and start wearing a lie. She knew that I knew what it meant, or could mean, but I didn't say anything.

"Where was your mum from?" she asked.

"Donegal. Gweedore. What about yours?"

"Galway. Oranmore."

"In Oranmore, in the County Galway, one

pleasant evening in the month of May," I started singing.

She smiled.

"I bet that's not the first time someone's done that," I said.

"My daddy used to sing it to my mum. That was their song."

"It's a beautiful song."

She nodded and I knew at that moment she wasn't in the café but somewhere else, a family party perhaps, sitting on the floor at her mum's knee as the room hushed and her daddy sang the song which spoke of a love that he'd never be able to say in words, his eyes glazed with tears that he'd blame on the drink if anyone said anything; her mum's eyes closed as she smiled and swayed to the music, letting her daughter's hair run through her fingers like water.

"I'm Eamon, by the way," I said, holding out my hand.

"Nice to meet you, Eamon by the way."

I smiled as I shook her hand which was small and rough and cold, and which disappeared inside my palm.

"I'm Deirdre."

"Hi, Deirdre.

"I know it's a horrible name and I hate it because everyone just thinks of Deirdre Barlow whenever I tell them."

"Who's Deirdre Barlow?"

"Are you kidding?"

"No."

"You don't know who Deirdre Barlow is?"

"Is she famous?"

"From Coronation Street. She wore giant glasses

that covered her whole face. She was married to Ken Barlow like about a dozen times."

"I'm only kidding. I know who Deirdre Barlow is."

"Very funny."

"But I still think it's a nice name."

Deirdre frowned.

"And you're a lot prettier than her."

She blushed and so did I. I don't think I'd ever used the word 'prettier' in my life before and I had no idea where it had come from. The door opened and we both looked round gratefully. A boy and a girl walked in, holding hands. They both looked about eighteen. He'd obviously not shaved for a week or two, hoping the growth would make him look older. She had odd shoes on – a pair of baseball boots – one green and one red. He whispered something in her ear and she laughed like it was the funniest thing she'd ever heard. I hoped the boy would bottle up that moment and treasure it forever.

"Sorry, we're closed."

The two of them stopped and looked at Deirdre.

"Okay," the girl said with a smile. She opened the door, leading the way as they stepped back outside, still holding hands.

Deirdre walked over to the door and pushed the lock, snapping the door shut. In the frame of the glass the boy and girl were kissing. He was much taller and was leaning down towards her as her hands clasped the back of his neck. She was on her tip-toes. It was like we were at an art gallery, studying a portrait in an exhibition called 'All You Need Is Love'.

When she walked back to the table Deirdre wore a smile that I couldn't decide was happy or sad or envious or just tired. I smiled back at her.

"Do you want another coffee?" she said.

"I thought everything was switched off for the night?"

"I can stick the kettle on."

"That would be nice."

She took the cup off me and put it behind the counter before disappearing through the door, reappearing a few moments later with a kettle which she plugged in. Immediately I could hear the hiss of the element as it began to heat up the water. She took off her overall and folded it several times until it was just a small purple square on top of the counter. I noticed that on the end of the silver chain was a small cross which sparked when she moved as the light caught it.

"You'll have to make-do with coffee," she said. "We're all out of cake."

Is There Something I Should Know

Once I had unwrapped all my other presents – a Primark shirt, some deodorant, a mug that read 'Life Begins at 48', and a large box of Maltesers – Rachel gave me the final present, handing it over so delicately I thought it must be made of glass. It was wrapped in paper that had 'BIRTHDAY BOY' printed all over it, in between images of a teddy bear playing football or tennis or driving a motor car.

"I hope you like it," she said, her face a mixture of make-up and expectation.

"I'm sure I will."

I tore open the wrapping paper to reveal a long, thin, brown box that was just a bit longer than a normal-sized ruler. As I turned it over in my hands, I could hear something rolling about inside. Rachel smiled and raised her eyebrows. I was tempted to prolong her agony but she looked to be on the point of snatching the box off me and opening it herself, so I opened the lid and turned the box upside down.

A drumstick slid out and landed on my palm. I looked up at Rachel, and then quickly scanned the room in case I'd missed the set of drums she'd bought to accompany the stick.

"It's Roger Taylor's drumstick," she said.

"Really?"

"It's signed too. I hope you like it."

I let it rest in my hand, rolling back and forth like a lazy wave, catching glimpses of the signature with every blink of my eyes. I wondered what record he'd played on with this stick. Maybe it was from the last album and he'd discarded it in the studio once the recording sessions had been finished, only to be picked up and put on eBay by an opportunistic sound engineer; I hoped it was older than that, though, a piece of genuine Duran Duran memorabilia from their first album or maybe even the Rio recordings. I didn't want to get my hopes up, though.

"There should be a certificate of authentication inside the box," Rachel said, reading my mind.

I handed her the drumstick and then put my forefinger into the box. There was a sheet of paper inside and I slowly prised it out, dropping the box on to the chair and unravelling the paper. I read it and re-read it, looking up at Rachel, who smiled, before reading it again. I handed the sheet of paper to her.

"It's Roger Taylor of Queen's drumstick," I said, snatching up my box of Maltesers and walking through to the kitchen.

ABOUT THE AUTHOR

Paul Cuddihy is a Duran Duran fan, and has been every since he first heard *Planet Earth* back in 1981. He was fourteen at the time. He is considerably older now, and maybe even a little wiser, yet he still remains a devoted Duranie (And, no, that's not Cockney rhyming slang!)

If he had to choose just one Duran Duran song for his Desert Island Discs, it would be *Save a Prayer*. If he was allowed two, then he'd also opt for *Secret Oktober*.

Made in the USA
Charleston, SC
07 August 2015